ANIMAL WIFE

ANIMAL WIFE

◆ ◆ ◆

stories

Lara Ehrlich

2018
Red Hen Press
Fiction Award

Red Hen Press | *Pasadena, CA*

Animal Wife
Copyright © 2020 by Lara Ehrlich
All Rights Reserved

Book design by Mark E. Cull

Library of Congress Cataloging-in-Publication Data

Names: Ehrlich, Lara, 1981– author.
Title: Animal wife : stories / Lara Ehrlich.
Description: First edition. | Pasadena, CA : Red Hen Press, [2020]
Identifiers: LCCN 2020025808 (print) | LCCN 2020025809 (ebook)
| ISBN 9781597098847 (trade paperback) | ISBN 9781597098830 (epub)
Classification: LCC PS3605.H7574 A6 2020 (print) | LCC PS3605.H7574
  (ebook) | DDC 813/.6—dc23
LC record available at https://lccn.loc.gov/2020025808

Publication of this book has been made possible in part through the financial support of Ann Beman.

The National Endowment for the Arts, the Los Angeles County Arts Commission, the Ahmanson Foundation, the Dwight Stuart Youth Fund, the Max Factor Family Foundation, the Pasadena Tournament of Roses Foundation, the Pasadena Arts & Culture Commission and the City of Pasadena Cultural Affairs Division, the City of Los Angeles Department of Cultural Affairs, the Audrey & Sydney Irmas Charitable Foundation, the Kinder Morgan Foundation, the Meta & George Rosenberg Foundation, the Albert and Elaine Borchard Foundation, the Adams Family Foundation, the Riordan Foundation, Amazon Literary Partnership, and the Mara W. Breech Foundation partially support Red Hen Press.

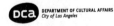

First Edition
Published by Red Hen Press
www.redhen.org

ACKNOWLEDGMENTS

The stories in this collection first appeared in the following publications, sometimes in slightly different form:

Boston Literary Magazine: "Kite"; *Columbia Review*: "Beware the Undertoad"; *Fiction Southeast*: "Animal Wife Revisited"; *F(r)iction*: "The Vanishing Point"; *HOOT*: "Paint by Number"; *Hunger Mountain*: "Animal Wife"; *Literary Orphans Journal*: "Stone Fruit"; *Massachusetts Review*: "Burn Rubber"; *Normal School*: "Night Terrors"; *Paper Darts*: "The Tenant"; *River Styx*: "Six Roses"; *SmokeLong Quarterly*: "Foresight"; *StoryQuarterly*: "Desiree the Destroyer"; *U.S. 1 Worksheets*: "Crush."

THANK YOU

To Immy, the best thing in my life. To Pamela Ehrlich, for always reading me just "one more story." To Brian Ehrlich, for "Billy Goats Gruff." And to Brenna Ehrlich Enos, for our childhood. To fearless, fabulous Sophia Macris. To Austin Gilkeson, greatest living Tolkien expert, and Oline Eaton, kindred spirit. To Abby Pekar, Blair Hurley, and Kirsten Arnett, who set the literary bar. To Manuel Gonzales, Liz Bergstrom, Andrew Mitchell, Erin Osborne, Meghan Purvis—and all the Killer Robots to whose strangeness I aspire. To Elizabeth McCracken, Amanda Boldenow, Rickey Fayne, Erica Hussey, Natalie Serber, and Lindsay Tigue for encouraging me to "go full deer." To Janice Checchio, for ferocity. To the Midwest Writers Workshop, StoryStudio Chicago, Grub Street in Boston, the Tin House Writers' Workshop, the Bread Loaf Writers' Conference, Martha's Vineyard Institute of Creative Writing, Wellspring House in Massachusetts, and the Snowed-in Residency at the Garret on the Green in New York. To the literary magazines that published these stories, and to Ann Hood for choosing *Animal Wife*. To everyone at Red Hen for their expertise, patience, and excellence, and Erin Harris of Folio Literary Management for unerring guidance. To Karen Chinca, for Immy. To Michelle Andelman, first reader of the pages that became *Animal Wife*. And to Douglas Riggs—FB—my ideal reader, my ideal everything.

For my mother. For Pamela.
For my daughter. For Imogen.

CONTENTS

Animal Wife   13

Night Terrors   35

Beware the Undertoad   41

Six Roses   65

Desiree the Destroyer   81

Crush   94

Foresight   95

The Vanishing Point   99

Kite   127

Burn Rubber   128

The Tenant   141

Paint by Number   145

The Monster at Marta's Back   146

Stone Fruit   157

Animal Wife Revisited   160

In villages where women bore most of the weight of a constricted life, witches flew by night on broomsticks or even on lighter vehicles such as ears of wheat or pieces of straw.

—Italo Calvino

ANIMAL WIFE

My father sits at the kitchen table with his shoulders hunched, staring at a feather cupped in his rough carpenter's hands. Its barbs are clean and white. The table is bare except for the box that held my mother's feathered robe. It is still encrusted with dirt. It has no latch, no key. My mother had to bash it open.

The kitchen is cold, and there is no dinner. Seventh grade ended today, so there is no homework. We sit across from each other in silence. I'm often restless, though I try not to be. "Young ladies should not fidget," my father always says. I will never be a lady.

I try not to fidget tonight and even sit up straight. There is dirt under my fingernails. I hide my hands in my lap so my father won't see, but he has forgotten I'm here. He just stares at the feather and doesn't say good night when I go upstairs to my room, my stomach growling.

There is a feather on my pillow. It glows white in the dark, the special kind of dark that makes you worry you've gone blind. When I was little and still afraid, my mother would lie with me, telling me story after story. Little girls who fell in love turned into sea foam or wind. They walked as if on knives, kept silent for seven years, wove thistle shirts until their fingers bled. They never learned to leave locked doors alone. Hunters and thieves and kings pursued them, carved out their hearts, scooped out their eyes, and snipped off their tongues. She told her own story like a fairy tale.

I do not brush my teeth tonight, since she is not here to make me. I cannot hear my father. Maybe he has fallen asleep at the kitchen table. The only sound is the house groaning as it settles.

My father built this house with his own hands. He learned to build from his father, who learned from *his* father, who made whaling ships. People came from miles around to watch my great-grandfather erect their giant ribcages on the shore. He sliced the trees into wide planks and laid them side by side. He ran rope between the boards so when they swelled with water, they wouldn't crack.

My father makes houses like boats, with wood and rope. He built our house for my mother over the pond where they met. He filled the pond with stones, a foundation for their love.

◆ ◆ ◆

There are scraping noises below my window. It is still dark, but I can just make out my father at the edge of the yard by the woods. He digs up the grass from the back door to the edge of the forest. He digs until our yard is a pit of stones surrounded by mountains of dirt.

My father thrusts his shovel under each stone and leans on the handle so hard it creaks. Finally, the stone sighs a puff of dirt and my father picks it up, bending his knees and keeping his back straight the way we learned to lift weights in gym class. It was the only useful thing I learned in gym class. He heaves the stones to the side along the tree line until they make a wall around the hole.

My father does not eat the sandwich I make for him. When I ask what he's doing, he just shakes his head, so I do not ask again. He doesn't seem to remember that he signed me up for ballet this summer, and I am not going to remind him. I pack my compass and canteen and slip into the woods.

My mother used to send me searching for what she called "objects of unexpected beauty," as though she didn't expect me to find beauty in Stone. But it is here, in the wide fields with crisscrossing stone walls—and the stones themselves. They seem so plain at first, but upon closer inspection there are threads of quartz glimmering through the granite. It's true that there's only so much to Stone, but I have walked the perimeter exactly 299 times, and I've discovered something new each time.

I used to bring my treasures to my mother—a stuffed bear with one eye, an hourglass with no sand. In the beginning, she pretended to admire my treasures, but as time passed, she stopped looking, until I no longer brought her anything. The box was different. When I offered it to my mother, her hands shook.

My mother said girls have to take care of themselves. That's how we avoid turning into sea foam and falling down wells. That's how we escape hunters and kings who chop and carve and snip and steal. That's why I practice punching every afternoon.

I got my boxing pad from Old Billy Brick, who works at the deli counter. The veins on the backs of his hands bulge like roots. He was a boxer, and his knuckles are calloused from breaking noses. I like to stare at them while he carefully slices the deli meat. One day, I will have hands like his.

There is a nail on the side of the house where I can hang my pad at punching level. The ground is eroded at the base of the wall here, like gums worn away at a tooth's root. The box was wedged between two exposed foundation stones. I dug for an hour to free it.

I do one hundred punches on one side, then a hundred more on the other. The first few weeks of training, my arms ached after twenty punches. Then fifty. Then seventy-five. Now I have calluses on the first two knuckles of each hand.

My father does not like the calluses. He says my bones are still growing. He does not understand that I have to take care of myself. "That's my job," he says, while he combs the tangles from my hair.

He has not combed my hair since the night before last, and the tangles may never come out. He has been digging without rest. His palms are blistered and bleeding. He's tired, but he is not weak. When Paul Cooper pushed me into the deep end and I couldn't make it to the edge, my father dragged me out. He threatened to kill Paul if he ever touched me again. Paul tripped me in gym the next day, but I didn't tell my father. I just punched him in the stomach, and he hasn't bothered me since.

When my knuckles are sore, I make my three-hundredth journey around Stone. It feels like time should have stopped when my mother left, but the town continues without us. People go about their lives, shopping for groceries and discussing car repairs in loud voices. The sidewalks and shop windows are too bright, as if it's just rained.

I return to the dirt and the stone walls and my father's silence. I help dig.

Digging is useful. I can feel my muscles tearing and reknitting stronger than before. I pretend I'm searching for treasure. I find a trove of shells that gleam in the sun. I find a skeleton with wing bones folded tight around a hollow heart space. The swan's long notched neck is graceful even in death.

My father won't let me keep it. He lifts it with his shovel and deposits it gently in the woods.

When the wall of stones has reached my waist, my father pries up a rock, and the earth below it becomes wet, the way blood wells up after a tooth is pulled. He shouts, and I drop my shovel. He spins me in circles, slipping in the mud. He has never had trouble lifting me before. His eyes are wide and his mouth is open as if he might laugh.

He digs with renewed purpose, though he won't say why. Blood runs down the shovel handle. I help him dig into the damp space, and by evening a pocket of what used to be our backyard is filled with water.

My father is still digging when I go up to bed without brushing my teeth. I haven't brushed them in three days, since my mother left. I lie on top of the sheets, guarding my treasures. It is too hot to sleep, and the shovel scrapes below my window.

Sometimes, when my mother didn't feel like telling stories, she would ask what I wanted to be when I grow up. An archaeologist. Geologist. Anthropologist. "What else?" she asked. Architect. Historian. "What else?"

She would lament that she had never accomplished anything, except having me. She wanted to be an artist, but had nothing to paint. My father suggested art classes at the community college, but the house would fall apart without her, she said.

She'd lie in bed beside me in the dark, and as she drew one finger between my eyes, she'd say, "You are the best thing in my life."

◆ ◆ ◆

My father is asleep on the steps with his head resting against the house. His legs are outstretched, his feet submerged in the pond that has engulfed our backyard. His face is tipped to the sun. His nose is peeling, and his cheeks are shadowed with stubble. When I sit beside him, he drags his eyes open, as if they are made of iron.

"Now she'll come home." His voice is rusty.

My father knows better than that. He knows my mother's stories as well as I do. One task is not enough to win her back. He must move a mountain with a silver spoon. Or plant an orchard in a single day. And when he finally finds my mother, he must keep his arms around her, even when she turns into a viper or fire or cloud of wasps. He must prove he deserves her.

The totems that guide a hero along a magical quest are as elusive as breadcrumbs. Knotholes disguise entries to other worlds. Wooden shoes take the hero bounding across the ocean. I keep my powers of observation sharp so I won't miss something and end up spitting toads.

Armed with my compass and canteen, and my mother's feather in a pouch around my neck, I scour the woods for enchantments. While my father is resting, I will discover the next task. It's my fault she left, after all.

I'm concentrating so hard I trip over the swan skeleton tangled in a nest of vines. Its neck bones have tumbled into a heap. They are smooth, as if worn by waves. I arrange them like a puzzle, except for the one I slip into my pouch with the feather.

A pebble glances off the top of my head, and a boy laughs in the branches.

"Who are you?" he calls down to me.

"Alex."

"That's a boy's name."

"No, it isn't. It's short for Alexandra."

He looks at me thoughtfully, without blinking.

"I'm Amir," he says. "You can come up, if you want."

I don't need his permission, but I'm good at climbing trees. I know just where to put my feet. The light sifts through the branches as though I'm underwater, climbing toward the sun.

Amir slides back on his branch to let me sit beside him.

"Most girls can't climb that well," he says.

His voice rises and falls. I know all about how boys' voices fly out of their control, which must be embarrassing.

"They could if they trained."

He raises one eyebrow, as if he's practiced in front of the mirror.

I can see everything from here: my father's pond, my father on the steps, the road running out to the highway. I can see all the secrets in a town that says it has no secrets.

"Did you hear about the bear bullet?" Amir asks. "Last week on I-90, two cars were driving from opposite directions, both going about eighty miles an hour—"

"Is this a math problem?" It's rude to interrupt, but I don't like math. I don't like questions about two trains coming from opposite directions and what time they would reach the station. In the real world, you'd just check the train schedule.

"Two cars were coming from opposite directions," he says, as if he hadn't heard me, "and a bear came loping out of the woods. "One car hit it and sent it flying like a bullet right through the windshield of the other car. *Whack!*" He slams his palms together. "A bear bullet."

"Was the bear okay?"

"Of course not."

His smugness is annoying, but my father says it's not polite for a young lady to point out other people's faults, especially when she has so many of her own.

"Have I upset you?" He looks a little nervous, as if I might cry. So, I tell him one of my mother's stories, about the Marsh

King who dragged a maiden down into the black mud to be his bride.

A smile cracks across his face. He unwinds a rope from the trunk, and a basket descends from the branches. He is well fortified. There are other ropes leading to a box of cookies, a flashlight, a bucket of rocks he calls missiles. He even has a net to trap intruders. He says I'm lucky he didn't use his net on me because he made it himself and it's strong enough to capture a full-grown man. He could live up here, if he had to.

Across the pond, my father stands and steadies himself against the house. His ribs poke through his shirt. He rubs his eyes with the heels of his palms like a little boy, but no one would dare pity him.

"What's wrong with him?" Amir asks, his eyes gentle with concern, as if he pities *me*.

"Nothing's wrong with him." I have my father's temper. My eyes bug out and a vein in my forehead twitches like a worm on a hook. Sometimes, I make myself mad on purpose, just to watch my face change.

"We're on a quest, and *you're* wasting my time." I shove back on the branch so fast I overturn one of his baskets, and missiles rain to the ground. Amir grabs my wrist.

"I'm sorry," he says, his voice soaring out of his reach. "If you tell me about it, I can help. I can teach you to make nets and launch missiles."

His fingers are hot. His eyes are green. My mother warned

me not to trust boys; they will take what they want without asking. But Amir can't take anything from me. I have calluses on my knuckles and scabs on my knees. I've made it to 110 punches without getting tired.

"I don't need help." I leap from the tree.

◆ ◆ ◆

This is the story my father tells: He was putting a roof on Old Billy Brick's house. You can see everything from a roof, like how the forest around Stone goes on forever. You can see all the secrets in a town that says it has no secrets.

From the roofs of Stone, my father saw the librarian kissing the pharmacist behind the grocery store. He saw Millie Rosewood sneak a cigar out of Old Billy Brick's pocket while he napped in his backyard. He saw Marcus White's fiancée break his heart, and he saw Marcus walk into the woods without a canteen or a compass. My father watched and watched, but Marcus never came out again.

My father saw many other fascinating things—but by far the most fascinating was my mother. He was sitting on the roof, eating his supper and looking for secrets, when he saw her, bathing in the pond.

My father stole through the trees to the water's edge. My mother had left her feathered robe on the ground, and he picked it up so it wouldn't get wet.

He says she wasn't embarrassed. She waded from the pond and held out her hand. And that is how my parents met.

When I asked my mother for her side of the story, she said nothing, only sighed.

◆　◆　◆

My stomach groans in my sleep. The house groans too, shuddering away from the water that laps at its sides. A film is closing over my father's pond, and mosquitoes hum above it like a storm cloud. My father waits on the back steps. He waits for the king of the birds, or the wise fish, or the wind. He waits for someone to tell him what's next.

When I ask why he's not eating his sandwich, he doesn't answer. He just stands in the shadow of the house, staring at the pond. Maybe he has sold his voice to the sea witch or taken a vow of silence.

He has deep wells below his eyes. I wrap my arms around his waist like I did when I was little. The mosquitoes whine above the pond. My father's heart beats against my cheek. I used to find his embrace reassuring.

He breaks free of my arms and staggers inside as if he has never walked before. The hallway light gleams off his scalp where his dark hair is wearing away. At the end of the hall behind the staircase, he shifts aside the chair that guards my mother's studio. It was a storage room, until the day he covered my mother's eyes and led her inside. He'd exchanged the boxes and cleaning supplies for a couch and an easel with a fresh canvas. He'd hung her favorite picture on the wall. In it, a woman stands at a window with her hips cocked, one foot tipped behind her. Her hair is tousled like she just woke up. All you can see out the window is water, as if the house were floating on the ocean.

My mother flung her arms around my father's neck, her dark hair falling loose. My father dipped his hands into it, as she looked up at him, smiling. I remember that smile because I saw it so rarely—when I asked for another bedtime story, when I brought her my first treasure.

My father closes the door behind him. The flies circle his uneaten sandwich. I should have kept my arms around him.

I won't let the house fall apart. I wash my father's dish and sweep the dirt from the doorway. There is nothing left to do, and yet my mother was always harried. She washed the dishes and the laundry, and when the dishes and the laundry were finished, she mopped the floor. By the time the floor was dry, there was more laundry, and then dinner and more dishes. Endless chores kept her from leaving the house, until her skin was so pale her veins shone through it like rivers.

A plank jumps beneath my feet. A moan shakes the foundation. The floorboards ripple from wall to wall, but the straining ropes hold them in place as they crack like knuckles. I press my eye to a knothole. Water glimmers below the floorboards. The spark of golden fish. The Marsh King's eyes glowing in the dark. There's a knock so loud I thump my forehead on the floor.

It's just Amir on the front steps. He holds out a bag of powdered donuts and asks if I'll teach him how to punch. The Marsh King moans deep under the house.

◆ ◆ ◆

Amir's fingers are long and narrow, and his nails are bitten down. My hands are not as quick—but they are stronger. He admires my calluses, and I teach him to keep his thumb folded over his knuckles as he punches. He leaves streaks of blood on my punching pad. Sweat runs into his eyes, and he asks me to tie a bandana around his forehead. My fingers fumble in his hair as I pull the knot tight.

While my father weaves shirts from nettles or spins flax into gold, Amir and I collect missiles. He shows me how to make a net that can capture a full-grown man. He doesn't tease me like the boys at school or tell me I don't act like a girl. He doesn't care that I haven't brushed my teeth in days. And he is a good audience for my mother's stories. He likes their darkness, full of wind and stolen voices.

Amir has heard the same stories—except the versions he knows have been milked of their poison. They have cartoon villains and happy endings. He likes mine better, he says, while his fingers knot the twine. In my mother's stories, the monsters are real.

The trunk warms my back. The branch grazes my thighs. My legs hang in the hot air as Amir pulls a picnic basket up through the branches. Sandwiches and lemonade and chocolate chip cookies. He smells like chalk on hot pavement.

"Do you believe in monsters?" he asks. His hands tighten on the rope. Our picnic swings in the sun.

"Of course."

"The Marsh King and the troll at the bridge, Rumpelstiltskin and the Undertoad—they're all the same," he says.

"I guess they could be."

When I close my eyes, the sun glows through my eyelids. I practice heightening my other senses. The hairs on my arms lift as the wind swings to the east. I feel the warmth of Amir's legs, so close to mine but not quite touching. If I listen hard enough, I might hear what the wind is saying.

"I've seen him," Amir says, hugging the branch with his knees as if afraid he'll fall.

"Who?"

"The Marsh King. He's as big as a bull and covered in warts. He eats children and pets, and his mouth is so wide he could swallow you whole. He waits below your bed, and under the stairs, and in the pool to drag you down by the ankles. And he's not always hiding. Sometimes, he'll sit at the kitchen table with a newspaper. Or wait in the truck, listening to the radio. He could be anywhere."

He weighs a missile in his palm.

The missiles are chunks of granite mottled with quartz. I slip one into my pouch with the feather and the bone. It knocks heavy against my chest.

I let Amir hold the feather, burning white against his sun-dark hands. He strokes the barbs with his fingertip so they separate and reseal in a neat row. He spins the feather between his fingertips, then tucks it behind my ear.

◆　◆　◆

Cracks spider up the walls. The Marsh King's eyes glow beneath the floorboards. He will not answer my questions.

Amir and I search for entrances to other worlds and the wooden shoes that take the hero bounding across the ocean. We trace the same old paths through the woods and collect missiles and weave nets, but nothing happens.

We wait on the back steps for the king of the birds, or the wise fish, or the wind. I don't know what's next. The day is empty and heavy. Amir stirs the water with his toes, sending lazy ripples against the house. My knee sweats where it presses against his, and our feet are ghostlike beneath the water. A mosquito alights on my wrist. Amir brushes it away, and the pressure of his fingers remains long after his touch.

The studio door is locked. I press my ear to the wood, and though I can't hear my father, I know he is hard at work. He needs to act faster. Soon, she will forget us.

◆ ◆ ◆

The darkness is so dense my eyes ache. My bed skates across the floorboards. My pictures tip off the walls as the house keels like a ship on a rough sea. It knocks me to my knees again and again as I stumble down the stairs and into the pond.

The water ripples from my steps in oily rings. Here, at the spot where my father hid the box, the house rises off its foundation. The pond has reclaimed the land beneath it. Between the house and the pond there is a sliver of space like a cavern at low tide. All this time, I've been peering into knotholes, while this must be the entrance to my mother's world. The cavern is just high enough for me to crawl inside.

"What are you doing?" Amir kneels beside me. He peers under the house, the planes of his shoulder blades lifting beneath his shirt. The mosquitoes swarm around us. The water soaks up my legs as I crawl into the cavern.

Amir grabs me around the waist. My shirt rides up, and his hands skid across the bare skin of my hips.

"Please." His fingers hook onto my hipbones. Everything rocks above me, open and ravaged. My mother warned me.

"Let's do something else," Amir says. "Something normal. We could go to a movie."

"No." Like knuckles on a punching pad. "I don't want you here."

Amir releases my waist. The pond is black and still as pavement. I almost apologize, but I'm not sure I should be sorry.

"I saw her," he says. His voice is thick, as if he's struggling against a spell compelling him to spit words like toads. "I was in the tree and I saw her, days ago. She came out of the house with a suitcase and got into a car on the corner, and she drove away. Your mother left, and you know it. Grow up, Alex."

A cloud of mosquitoes lifts around him as he splashes away, and I kneel in the greasy pond until he is gone.

A moan ripples through the water, more a vibration than a sound. The Marsh King crouches below the house, quivering with anticipation. He could swallow me whole.

My father does not answer my knock. The key to my mother's room still hangs on the kitchen hook. When I open the door, dust sifts through the air and settles over him. He is lying on my mother's couch with his face to the wall. The curtains are drawn. He does not move an inch. He does not make a sound. I hold my breath, afraid he might be dead, but I can just barely hear him breathing. The easel stands empty in the corner. My mother never bought paint.

There are no nettle shirts, no skeins of gold, no boots to

take a hero bounding across the sea. There is nothing except a man in a quiet room. All this time, my mother has been waiting, while my father has just been lying here. And instead of helping, I was playing with a boy.

The blood rushes in my ears. The vein in my forehead throbs. I press my hands against my father's back. He does not turn away from the wall.

"What about the quest?"

My voice hangs empty in the air.

◆ ◆ ◆

In my mother's stories, the maiden sinks through the swamp, through the ceiling of a crystal palace where toad servants clothe her in silken gowns. She tumbles down a well into a golden forest. She walks for seven days that feel like seven minutes. Oceans peel back like orange rinds. Her dress always stays clean.

The ground slopes beneath the house and the water deepens. I am not afraid. I have calluses on my knuckles and scabs on my knees. I've made it to 120 punches without getting tired. I have trained for this.

The ground drops away beneath my feet. It's so dark I can't tell whether my eyes are open or closed. My legs tingle with the brush of darting fish. The water trapped here is sluggish, sliding against my lips. Oily bubbles erupt against my cheeks.

The house's underbelly rasps the top of my head. The water is rising—or the house is sinking.

One last gasp of air, and then nothing but the weight of water on all sides. I hold my breath, pushing through the quiet and the cold. Though I kick, I'm no longer sure I'm moving, and there's no space to turn around. My lungs ache. No one knows I'm here.

The treasure pouch knocks against my chest. I fumble at the swollen knot. The feather, the missile—the bone. I press the bone between my lips, and air trickles into my throat.

Moans swell around me like whale calls. The water churns from below, thickening with mud that drags along my arms. It forces my legs together. Talons dig into my ankle, and the Marsh King yanks me down. He spins me like an alligator rolls its prey. My head slams the underside of the house. Colors burst behind my eyes. I grip the bone between my teeth and wrestle Amir's missile from the pouch.

I draw my knees to my chest, making myself small, and smash the missile hard between my feet. A groan thrums through my bones. The shock of it jumps in my eyes like tears, and the grip on my ankle loosens. I strike again and again, turning the water coppery, kicking until his grip releases. His groans thunder through my stomach. Water pours up my nose, burning my throat. My heart drums in my ears. My knees scrape stone.

The ground slants upward. The water lowers, and I breathe

deeply again, emerging onto the bank of a lake surrounded by pines as tall as masts. Stars peer through branches. The night smells like pine, rainwater, the musk of bears. When I wade from the lake, my clothes are dry. The sun hangs in the treetops, turning the forest gold.

A blizzard of feathers darkens the sky. Twelve swans swarm the bank of the lake, their eyes sharp with suspicion. They circle me, swiping at my ankles with their beaks.

I should recognize my mother by the way she holds her head or the slant of her eyes. They fix me with an unblinking gaze, their necks weaving like snakes. But I do not know her. I don't know what she wanted before she met my father, or why she stayed with us so long. I don't know what she would have painted, or who she would have been.

They crowd me, striking my sides, my arms, my thighs, leaving angry stripes on my skin. One rears back, revealing a bare patch just inside her left wing.

The feather is still in my pouch. Its barbs are clean and white. I place it before her, pointed at her breast.

The swans fall still. My skin throbs where the marks are turning blue. The swans enfold me and press their bodies close. The one with the bare patch lays her head in my lap. I curl my fingers around her neck and close my eyes.

"I'm here to bring you home," I say.

She turns cold, contracting into coils sliding around my waist. Then she expands, her scales shifting to thick, hot fur.

She grows until my arms cannot reach around her. She thrashes and bites, slicing my skin, but I cling to her and do not cry out. She breaks into a swarm of hornets, and I gather them in my arms, even as they drive their needles into my chest.

The hornets collapse in on themselves. The sting dissolves. My arms are empty.

Fingers trace my forehead, my eyelids, my tears. I was the best thing in her life, she said. I keep my eyes closed tight, memorizing her touch even as it fades.

The beat of wings forces me to my knees among the leaves churning across the forest floor. The trees thrash in anger. The wind rebels on my behalf, but the swans are stronger. They rise, sweeping toward the pines. Her long neck arches as if in pain. Her mournful call shivers as it is whipped away by the wind.

The sun casts her shadow on the pond. Her feathers stand out in relief, like the prints I used to make in school by resting an object—a coin, a key—on paper. The sun burns the world away around each feather, leaving it imprinted in negative space.

NIGHT TERRORS

When Lydia was ten, she stood on an overturned barrel in the woods and proclaimed herself king. The barrel splintered, and Lydia's foot plunged through, soaking her leg in greasy rainwater, grazing her shin along the bone. She skirted the garden where her mother was sweet-talking the tomato plants that never bore fruit. She burrowed under her covers, breathing in and out, and as her alarm faded, the familiar shame crept in. She confessed ten minutes later.

"It's my fault," Lydia's mother said as the doctor administered a tetanus shot. "I didn't warn you about standing on rotten barrels in the woods."

Now that Lydia is thirteen, she no longer plays in the woods surrounding her house on the farm that is no longer a farm. At the end of the long dirt driveway there are two granite pillars that once held a gate, but there is no gate. There is a toolshed with no tools. Inside the toolshed, there are chickens: four bantam hens and a rooster too puzzled to fertilize them.

Lydia doesn't mind that there are no eggs. The chickens sleep in her lap like cats. Her favorite hen is pure white with feather dusters bursting from her heels. When Lydia's school bus stops between the granite pillars, her chicken shoots from the forsythia bush and up the long driveway as Lydia's classmates cheer her on.

Every evening, the chickens file out of the bush and into the shed. Lydia drops the latch and presses her ear to the door, listening to their quiet rustling. Every morning, she tidies their sawdust nests and checks for eggs. There are never eggs.

Lydia's bedroom window overlooks the shed backed by the woods where she once was king. The farmhouse and surrounding woods are swathed in darkness punctured only by pinhole stars.

What was that sound? She awakens to an echo. Just the house settling, or a loon in the swamp beyond the woods. The loons scream like women. Their screams shiver and die on the wind. The sheet has twisted around her legs, and when she peels it from her nightgown, static sparks against her skin. What if someone were dying out there, and she just pulled the covers over her head?

Headlights burn through the trees. Lydia holds her breath, willing the lights to fade. But what if they turned down the long driveway, casting the farm in a milky glow—only to cut off below her window? Then, in the expectant darkness and the silence of the farm that is no longer a farm, someone might murder her family.

What was that sound? Lydia leans out the window, holding her breath. She can just make out the driveway below, and the shed where the chickens are roosting. In the raw silence, the echo fades from her memory until she can't be certain she heard it at all. She turns her pillow and rests her cheek against the cool side.

But what if the murderer knows there's a farmhouse at the end of the long driveway? What if he knows that they don't have a dog, only a shed full of chickens? He might cut the engine between the granite pillars. He might drape a towel over his shoulder and rest a shotgun against the towel. He might stroll down the long driveway, his work boots jangling in the dark, all the way to the end where the house creaks in its sleep.

When she was small and had woken in the night, she had tiptoed to her parents' room. She had forced herself to walk slowly because the school librarian had not been careful and slipped down the stairs in the middle of night. Her husband told the papers he'd awoken to the sound of her neck cracking like a gunshot.

Lydia had tiptoed down the hallway, guided by her father's snores. She had opened her parents' door a sliver and whispered, "Mommy," panic lifting the end of her voice. The snores had cut off, and her father's Big Bad Wolf growl had rumbled from the cave of the bedroom: "What is it?"

"I heard a noise." Once she had pushed her fears through her parents' door, she could breathe again. If they were murdered in the night, at least it wouldn't be her fault.

Her mother had understood, because she, too, worried about murderers and rain barrels and steep staircases. It's natural to worry, her mother had explained as she tucked Lydia back into bed. Our great-great-grandmothers worried because they had to be ready to run from mammoths. The mammoths died long ago, but the fear settled deep into our bones.

When Lydia turned thirteen, her mother said it was time she learned to comfort herself. She gave Lydia the string of worry beads she had inherited from her own mother. Lydia keeps them on the bedpost.

What was that sound? A loon's scream. A door slam. A footfall on the porch steps.

She unloops the beads from the post and slides them along the string one at a time. Just this week, there was a story on the news about a man in Cleveland who had kept a woman chained in his bedroom. His neighbors heard the woman screaming, but told themselves it was the wind. "That woman got into a stranger's car," Lydia's mother had said, and turned off the TV. "You know better."

Lydia slides the beads along the string. Static sparks against her skin as she pulls back the blankets. She opens her door just enough to squeeze through, and tiptoes down the hallway.

Another news story: In Florida, a little girl had awoken her parents. "I heard a noise," she'd whispered. Her mother had understood, because she, too, heard noises in the night. The doors were locked, but there was a snapping, scraping sound just outside, like a huge animal dragging something along the ground. Her mother pulled back the curtain. In the glow of the porch light, the driveway was caving in. They made it across the street just in time to watch the ground devour their house from garage to swimming pool. What if that little girl had just pulled the covers over her head? Lydia's mother had stroked her hair and said, "We don't have sinkholes in Connecticut."

Lydia holds her breath at the top of the stairs. The only sound is the rumble of her father's snores. The beads grind against her finger bones. If the little girl had not woken her parents, they all would have skated into the earth, still tucked in their beds, and it would have been her fault.

The responsibility is dizzying. Lydia longs to push her fear through her parents' door so she can breathe again. But she is no longer a little girl. She slides a bead along the string. There is no murderer. She slides a bead along the string. There is no woman screaming. She slides a bead along the string. There are no sinkholes in Connecticut. She turns at the top of the stairs, carefully, so she does not fall.

In the morning when Lydia unlatches the toolshed, the chickens do not greet her. The sawdust is strewn with white feathers turned red. The chickens had slept in her lap like cats. Lydia's mother says there is nothing she could have done once the weasel got in. But Lydia vows never to let her guard down again.

She finds the barrel in the woods where she once was king. Rainwater glistens in the hole her foot had plunged through. She drops the worry beads into the hole and listens. They sink without a sound.

BEWARE THE UNDERTOAD

My grandmother made me strip my bathing suit on the doormat just inside her kitchen. Balancing stork-like, shedding sand, I struggled to free my ankle from the suit strap. The door opened behind me. My hands flew up, though I had nothing to cover yet, and then down. I couldn't hide all of myself at once. The neighbor boy was standing there, his eyes huge behind his glasses. Time stretched and slowed. And stopped. I let him look.

"You were so fat," David would say a few summers later, grown out of his embarrassment. "You had sand in your rolls." He would pinch my side. Maybe he was cruel. But the crueler he was, the more I prized his moments of tenderness, pocketing them like stones.

At the start of each summer I spent at the sea, I found David by the flash of his hair in the sun. He never burned, except for the patch between his shoulder blades. I followed him over the rocks that formed three spokes radiating out to sea, diminishing until they sank beneath the surface. When my grandmother was a girl, she and her friends had jumped from stone to stone, until the boy she'd loved had cracked his head open. The water had danced away with his blood.

David showed me how to smash a snail just hard enough to shatter its shell and keep its body intact. He cut a length of string for me, and though my fingers were slick with snail, I pulled the knot tight around it.

Water sloshed in the crevices between the rocks. We lowered our snails until they struck the water and he showed me how to tug the string to mimic the flutter of prey. Our heads tipped together. The sun warmed our necks. When the string began to vibrate, I drew up a blue crab with my snail clamped in its claws. Its exoskeleton glistened, reminding me of stars.

"That's a good one!" David flipped the crab onto its back.

It had the broad abdomen of a female and the red-tipped claws my Audubon guide called "painted fingernails." Its Latin name, *Callinectes sapidus*, means "savory beautiful swimmer," I told David, and the females mate only once. We studied the crab together, tracing the contours of her underbelly. She clawed at us like she was drowning.

The summer kids were a tribe. Holding hands in a chain, we raced down the beach and dropped to our knees in the sea foam, shrieking, "The Undertoad's got me!"

The Undertoad's spit fizzed at our knees, speckled with bits of the fish and crabs and children he'd eaten. "Look, there's a finger!" Beware the Undertoad that crouches between the shallows and the deep where the sand drops off below your feet. He is as big as a bull, and his greasy hide is puckered with warts. His milky eyes strain through the gloom. As he devours eels and lobsters and stingrays, his body balloons to twice its girth, quivering as he digests. His mouth is so wide the corners almost meet behind his head. He could swallow you whole.

We dared each other to swim to the raft but stopped where the sand slopes toward the deep. The Undertoad waits for you to push away from the edge and tread suspended, kicking against the sea. Then, he catches your ankle and drags you down through the dark and the cold.

David collected sea glass in jam jars. Each shard was from a bottle that had smashed against the rocks and had been worn smooth by the sand and sea. The bottles once held secret messages, he said. Treasure maps and spy codes. And love letters, I said.

We sat cross-legged on his crumpled sheets. Though the window was open, the curtains hung slack, and moths sailed in to orbit the bedside lamp. Our grandmothers were talking in the next room, their voices like waves. We still wore our bathing suits and seawater had dried on our skin. If you licked your arm, I showed David, your lips puckered.

"I'll tell you a joke," he said. "A little girl was walking home from school with her arms full of books, when a man came up to her on the sidewalk.

"'Those books look heavy,' the man said. 'I'll carry them if you let me put my finger in your belly button.'

"She let him carry her books.

"At the end of the street, the man said, 'Now you owe me,' and led her into the bushes. He set her books on the ground.

"'Hey!' she said. 'That's not my belly button!'

"And he said, 'That's not my finger.'"

I woke to my grandmother stroking my hair. I lay beside David under the sheets. Our legs were pressed together, sticky with salt and sweat. My bathing suit straps bit into my sunburnt shoulders.

My grandmother took my hand and led me outside and down the stone path to her house, through the cattails that stood taller than our heads. She squeezed my hand and said, "We won't tell your mother."

It seemed I should be ashamed of something, but I didn't know what.

The summer girls pressed around me on the rocks as I whispered into their flushed faces, my voice low and halting.

"A little girl was walking home from school with her arms full of books, when a man came up to her on the sidewalk."

What had the man done to the girl behind the bushes? We searched for clues in the punch line, but every word introduced another mystery.

Our summer tribe discovered new lands and made them our own. Tír na nÓg emerged beyond the raft at low tide. A deer had paced there once as the waves grappled for her hooves. We waited at the salt lick for the Antler King. We built houses for the little people on the moss path. The loon's call sounded like a woman screaming. The shipwreck was our battlefield. It sagged at one end of the beach, and the restaurant it had been was long since closed. Its heavy carpet soaked up the water from our bare feet and never dried.

We met at the wreck when it stormed. There was no secret signal. We saw the storm coming, and we came with it. We pressed against the railing, leaning into the rain as it pushed across the ocean like a curtain swinging shut.

We marched beneath the eaves and the raindrops parted our hair. We called it eavesdropping. When we were good and soaked, we ran down the beach and into the sea spray, shrieking, "The Undertoad's got me!" We dared each other to swim to the raft but stopped at the boundary between the shallows and the deep, comfortable with our cowardice.

We came to dinner with sand between our toes. Every meal seemed to last forever. While the grownups finished their coffee and conversations, we waited on the back steps until their voices drifted into silence.

David's grandfather emerged from the house and walked past us without a backward glance. When he reached the driveway, he growled over his shoulder, "What are you waiting for?" and we scrambled after him and piled into his pickup.

When we were very small, two of us could fit on the front seat and David's grandfather tucked a blanket across our knees. Though David was the grandson, he didn't have special privileges; sometimes he would ride in front with his grandfather and sometimes in back with the garbage pails.

The logging path curved beyond the headlights. David's grandfather drove with his elbow resting on the open windowsill, steering with just his knuckles. My leg pressed against David's under the blanket. When I looked over my shoulder through the cabin window, I could just make out the others huddled in the truck bed like stowaways. A hint of garbage drifted in through the window.

His grandfather stopped the truck deep in the forest, and we handed the pails down to him. He upended them at the tree line and backed the truck a little way down the path. Then he cut the engine, and we waited.

Some nights, there was nothing. But if we were lucky, a mound of darkness shouldered through the trees. David's grandfather turned on the fog lights to reveal a black bear straddling the garbage heap. Unfazed, it nuzzled our trash, sorting through scraps with its paws, scooping leftover fish and cake and coffee grounds into its mouth. I had read that when *Ursus americanus* hibernate, their hearts slow to eight beats a minute, as if they can control time.

"They survived the Ice Age," I whispered to David.

"Maybe they hibernated until it was over," David whispered back.

Under the blanket, I held his hand. I wished he could come to my grandmother's house with me. We'd sit cross-legged in my room, our knees touching, and talk until we fell asleep. But I knew now that I should not invite boys into my bed.

Savory swimmer. Tír na nÓg. Undertoad. Antler King. Little people. Loon's call. The wreck. The raft. Cattails. Hunting snails. Summer girls. Sandy sheets. The bear. Sea glass in jam jars. David's eyes widening. His knee against mine. The warmth of his hand.

I invoked every detail on the train ride home, preserving the summer in my memory before it slipped down the tracks behind me. Soon enough, home would become real again. I would wear a uniform. I would walk to school, past the dry cleaner and the convenience store and the other dry cleaner. I would practice clarinet. I would speak when called upon. I would do homework in my bedroom while my parents fought in the kitchen. I would live the rest of the year for summer.

Upon returning home, I was always alarmed that life had continued without me. My parents had painted the living room. Our cat had died. My best friend had kissed a boy. Or, he had kissed her. Such distinctions mattered at twelve.

"Our teeth scraped," she said with an embarrassed laugh.

My shoulder blades shuddered against the headboard. She picked at her fingernails, chipping polish onto her bedspread.

I was sorry for her. Kisses were for the ends of books and the finales of films. Those were the good kisses, the ones that led to happily ever afters. Stories never start with a kiss.

One by one, my friends kissed boys we had known since we were born. We had napped together in nursery school. We had fed each other paste in kindergarten and exchanged valentines in first grade. Now, they paired off in the hallway, broke up at lunch, and took up with someone else on the walk home.

I would not let this happen to me. I would be seduced by a charming man who had never eaten paste. I would hold his hand on a moonlit beach. We would dance slow, and though he might try to sweep his hands lower, I would not let him. I would not waste my first kiss on a boy who chewed erasers. My friends could not convince me otherwise, and when school ended, I was glad to leave them behind.

"Who is this beautiful woman on my doorstep?" my grandmother asked and hugged me so tight my arms went numb.

Her frayed corduroys swished as she led me down the hall to my bedroom. My sheets smelled like lavender. The sound of the ocean poured through my window, far from the traffic. The clock in my grandmother's kitchen told the time in days.

I found David by the flash of his hair in the sun. I cradled a shard of sea glass against my thumb. It was deep blue, the rarest color, he had said. Pirate's glass. What had the bottle held? A treasure map or a secret code. A love letter.

He seemed to have grown three feet since last summer. His hair curled at his neck. His eyes turned to mine, then fell away. Speaking suddenly seemed precarious. My voice would come out too high, or I would say the wrong thing, and there would be no taking it back.

The sand shifted under my heels as he passed behind me, and I pulled my towel tight across my chest.

The summer boys enveloped him and stampeded down the beach. I followed with the girls. When we reached the waves, we dropped to our knees in the foam shrieking, "The Undertoad's got me!" still half-convinced he was real.

The boys huddled at the bow of the wreck, their ears against the cabin wall. When I came around the corner, they started like jackrabbits. I edged in beside David to press my ear against the wood.

I heard a murmur of voices. A heavy breath, a pitched

moan, as if someone were in pain. David's cheek was pressed beside mine, and my face was warm against the wood.

"Do you know what they're doing?" he whispered. He was so close that I could see sand in his eyebrows.

I knew enough to realize there was plenty I didn't know. The romances I read ended with a chaste kiss on the stairs, the promise of passion beyond the book covers. I had learned about sex from a video in health class. While the boys followed the teacher—who was also the football coach—to the locker room, the girls sat cross-legged behind the climbing rope. In the video, a girl got her first period during a sleepover and her mother taught the girls about menstruation by making pancakes shaped like ovaries.

I feared my period would strike when I was least expecting it, so I tried to expect it, always.

"Have you ever seen a naked man?" David leaned closer still.

His eyes were as blue as the pirate glass. I tried to stare him down, to maintain an expression of indifference, but my lips trembled with the effort. I studied the wall, picking at a splinter.

"I've seen you naked." He pinched my side. "You were so fat, with sand in your rolls."

His fingers rasped my skin. His breath smelled like cigarettes. I pushed away from the wall and stomped down the deck, making as much noise as I could. I looked back only when I reached the woods. The boys had scattered, and the beach was quiet. I sat on the Antler King's log to wait.

One of the summer boys emerged from the wreck. He carried his shirt wadded in his fist and strode away without looking back. A few minutes later, a summer girl struck off across the beach in the opposite direction. Even from the woods, I could see that her eyes were dark and wet.

The summer girls stopped eavesdropping. They stopped swimming and began sunbathing in bikinis instead. I did not miss them. When I was alone, I felt everything more deeply. I felt with my nerves and the hairs on my arms. I felt my heart straining against my skin, and I had to press it back. When I was alone, I could convince myself that David's mockery concealed a depth of passion he was not yet ready to plumb.

At night, I aimed the fan at my head. Lifting the screen did nothing to ease the heat. I dreamed he would come to my window, like in the fairy tales. "Can I come in? I won't make a sound." He would climb onto my bed, strewing sand across my sheets. We would sit cross-legged with our knees touching and talk until we were half-asleep. Then I would pull the sheet over us. We would share my pillow, our faces so close in the dark that I would feel his breath on my lips. He would be my first kiss, I decided. He had already seen me naked.

The boys dared each other to swim to the raft, showing off for the girls, who sunbathed on the beach, sleek and glossy as seals. They turned their faces away, feigning disinterest. The ocean slid up my stomach and over my breasts. It licked my collarbone. The raft bobbed at an unimaginable distance. If I could just reach it, I knew, everything would go back to the way it should be.

I pushed toward the slope, where the sand was deep and thick. Weeds coiled around my ankles as I passed through pockets of warm water where the ocean had trapped the sun. The raft drifted just beyond the Undertoad's lair. The girls rolled onto their stomachs and untied their bikini tops as the boys taunted one another louder. The sea brushed up my neck, slid over my chin, and pressed against my mouth. The sand sloped beneath my feet. I closed my eyes.

The Undertoad was waiting. I could sense him worming closer. His body rippled with anticipation. His webbed fingers twitched toward my toes. They would slide up my ankle, my shin, my thigh, until one long, webbed finger would hook me like a trout. I could go no further. I stood suspended on the slope in a one-piece suit.

David kicked past me. The boys cheered him on as he passed through the open space where the Undertoad was waiting. His head dipped and reappeared, his hair gleaming in the sun. He swam further than any of us had gone, out where the waves were razors.

"The Undertoad isn't real," I told myself as the rain pushed across the ocean. It darkened the raft and steamed up the sand. The girls scrambled to their feet, their bikini straps trailing, and huddled under their towels to watch as David heaved onto the raft. He rolled onto his back, staring up at the sky. We cheered until he sat up, grinning, and gave us the finger.

He lounged out there all day like a king, reminding us that he was brave, and we were beach-bound.

I got my period at high tide. When I finally confessed to my grandmother, she sat me down at the kitchen table. We are descended from the moon, she explained. It was part of the earth until it broke away and spun into space. Water filled the hole it left behind, and that's why the ocean breathes in and out with the moon. All organisms began as cells made of seawater, and we brought it with us when we climbed onto land. We each carry an ocean inside us.

I was finally allowed to have a two-piece, but it was baby blue with daisies, and the front sagged. My grandmother promised it would fill out soon enough, but I didn't believe her.

The girls left the beach. They walked into town, where they hung out at the gas station that also sold groceries, videos, and live bait. They dared each other to buy things from the older boy who worked behind the counter and wait at the pump for him to come out for a smoke. He told them dirty jokes, and they laughed and shook their hair over their sun-burnt shoulders.

The boys swam out farther, reaching the raft one by one, until I was alone on the beach with my little sister. It was Hannah's first summer at the sea, and she would not go near the water, for fear of the Undertoad. He liked little girls best, David had said. She was six and entitled to her fear. I had no excuse. I pretended I'd rather sunbathe and reclined on my stomach with my ankles crossed in the air. I arched my neck. It was difficult to read that way.

Hannah squatted in the sand. Her hair had come loose from its braid and feathered around her head. Her giraffe inner tube watched from the far end of her towel, smiling with his painted lips. She took him everywhere, but refused to swim.

"Hannah, come in with me," David called from the ocean. "The Undertoad's hungry!"

He had called out to me, once.

Hannah shook her head, and he jogged up from the ocean, his trunks plastered to his thighs. He scrubbed his hands through his hair and flicked his fingers at me, splattering my book. He did not apologize. He sat next to Hannah and put on her pink sunglasses shaped like stars. I turned a page.

"What are you making?" he asked Hannah, who was digging a hole.

"A hole," she said.

I envied how she still said exactly what she meant.

"Want to swim with me?"

She shook her head and clamped the giraffe under one arm.

"You don't need him," David said. "I'll keep you safe from the Undertoad."

She gripped the giraffe tighter. "I don't believe in the Undertoad."

My face wavered in the sunglasses. As clouds passed over the beach, wiping away my reflection, I could just make out David's eyes, and I was certain he was staring at me—until the sun emerged again and burned away my certainty.

Hannah dragged her pail down the beach to the wet sand, stranding David and me across the hole. My face faded in and out of the glasses.

"Quit staring at me," he said.

"I wasn't!"

"It's okay. I stared at you once, too." He reached across the hole to pinch my side. "You were so fat, with sand in your rolls." His sandy fingers rasped my skin. I sat up and pulled in my legs, hiding my white thighs with my book. Hannah scooped heavy sand into her bucket.

"What are you reading?" He pushed the sunglasses to the top of his head and leaned in to read my book's faded title.

"Tennyson."

"What's that?"

"Poetry."

"I had to read a poem for English last year. It was crap." His hair fell across his eyebrows, hiding his expression. "Do you have a boyfriend?"

"No," I said. I was aware of my sagging top, my bare stomach, and the razor burn trailing down my shins.

"Why not? What's wrong with you?" He nudged my foot with his. Heat coursed through my inflamed follicles. He propped his elbows on his knees and leaned in close. His eyes flicked to my forehead, my chin, my lips.

"Must be something wrong with you," he said. "You're not *that* ugly."

My heart beat in my ears as if the water were closing over my head. I crossed my arms over my stomach. His eyes returned to mine, and I could tell he was smiling though I wouldn't let myself look at his lips. I feared he could see the desire on me, like a sweat stain.

David sat on the rocks with a jam jar of tobacco between his feet and seagulls circling above his head. He licked the edge of a rolling paper and packed the tobacco tight. He struck his matches on a stone.

Sometimes a summer girl would sit beside him and set the jar between her feet, her pink toenails glistening. He'd show her how to lick the paper and pack the tobacco. She would light the cigarette and take a drag, and when she made a show of coughing, he would laugh. I would not have coughed. But I would not have rolled his tobacco for him, either.

I dreamed I saw the tip of his cigarette pulsing from my bedroom window. The only sound was Hannah's gentle snoring. I'd kneel and let the sheets fall from my waist. He would stare in at me, his cheeks red from the heat. It seemed he didn't care if I let him in or not. That's why I would let him in.

I'd unlatch the window and he'd help me slide it up, our fingertips touching. He'd climb onto my bed, strewing my sheets with sand. His face would be partially lit by the moon slanting through the open window. Lifting the screen would do nothing to ease the heat. Hot air would pour through in waves. Outside everything would be white and quiet and still.

"You were so fat, with sand in your rolls," he would whisper as his palm slid around my hip. The seawater would have dried on our skin. If you lick your skin, he'd show me, tracing his tongue along my collarbone, your lips pucker. I'd hold my breath as his tongue touched mine. He would taste like salt and cigarettes.

I constructed the fantasy from scavenged details, but I didn't know what should happen next. What would I do with my hands? What would he do with his tongue?

The ocean slid up my stomach and over my breasts. It licked my collarbone. Hannah watched me from her towel as I pushed toward the slope, where the mud was deep and thick. Seaweed coiled around my ankles.

I waved at Hannah, teasing her like David had, and she ran down the beach, the inner tube bouncing behind her on the sand. She stopped at the sea foam, seeking bits of the fingers the Undertoad had eaten.

David leapt off the raft with a bellow that rippled across the waves. The sea brushed up my neck, slid over my chin, and pressed against my mouth. The sand dropped away beneath my feet. I closed my eyes. All sound turned to static, and then there was nothing but the weight of water pressing from all sides. I entered a great yawning space.

I sank toward the Undertoad, daring him to catch me. I held my breath, drifting down through the quiet and the cold. There's no such thing as the Undertoad. I knew it, but my body wasn't convinced. I sensed him crouched at the bottom, straining to see through the silt to the sun glimmering on the surface high above. I was the passing shadow that signaled prey. "Go on," I dared him. "Go on and try."

A shadow bloomed out of the foggy deep and coiled around my ankle. I opened my mouth to scream, and water poured up my nose and into my throat. My heart beat in my ears. Salt seared my eyes. I thrashed in the monster's grip.

The pressure released, and I shot to the surface, kicking blindly. My nose was streaming and my throat burned. My shoulder scraped against the raft. Beside me, David was laughing.

"Just kiss him and get it over with," my best friend said, leaning back against the headboard. She gazed down at me with pity, and I buried my face in the blanket.

How could she understand? She had, by now, kissed three more boys and planned to have sex with one of them, though she hadn't decided which. I was still holding out for hand-holding. Roses. A film-finale kiss.

"You worry too much," she said. "He'll do whatever you want."

What had happened to her fear, to her quiet confession behind lowered lashes? She knew things now.

I concentrated on school and music and sports. I convinced myself I had forgotten David. But as the days grew warmer and the school year closed, I began planning what I'd say when I saw him again, wondering if he had cut his hair, if he had missed me, if he would notice how I'd changed. I was taller, thinner, maybe, and my eyes could be hard. I would look at him with scorn. I would tell him I loved him. I would tell him I never thought about him at all.

"Who are these beautiful women on my doorstep?" my grandmother asked and hugged Hannah and me until we squealed. Her frayed corduroys swished as she led us down the hall to our bedroom, where the sheets smelled like lavender. The sound of the ocean poured through the window.

I found David by the flash of his hair in the sun. I imagined pressing my palm against the sunburnt patch between his shoulder blades and soaking up the heat. The first sighting was always a physical shock, no matter how thoroughly I had prepared. He stripped my poise, returning me to myself, and I felt just as I had when standing naked before him on the kitchen mat.

His eyes turned to mine, then fell away. The sand shifted under my heels as he passed behind me. Though Hannah begged me to stay, I left my towel on the sand and followed him.

The raft no longer seemed so far away. I carved through the water without a thought to the Undertoad and pulled myself onto the boards after David. We lay side by side, our arms outstretched, our palms on the planks, radiating heat. My fingers itched to close the distance. The wood rose and fell beneath us, the only sounds the slop of the water against the underside of the raft and David's quick breath.

The heat soaked through my suit, which had filled out between summers, just as my grandmother had promised. I resisted the urge to wrap my arms across my chest and peeked at David.

His eyelids flickered as if under the strain of keeping them shut, and he was still, except for his breath running in and out, timed with the waves. I pressed my palm against my stomach and matched my breath to his.

The silence spread between us, hot as the air between our arms. The waves sucked at the wood, and when David's little finger grazed my thigh, goose pimples broke out along my legs. I stared at the sky, sagging with rain, and waited for him to laugh at my razor-burnt shins and bruised knees. He brushed my thigh again, and when he pressed his fingers there, the muscles in my leg jumped against his hand. His breath outpaced the water as time stretched and slowed.

His hot palm stuttered up my thigh. The sky was solid and heavy, pushing me down against the boards. He slipped his fingers inside my bathing suit.

Hannah watched from the beach, clutching her giraffe by the neck. I stared back, burning in her innocent gaze. He hadn't confessed his undying love. Hadn't held my hand on the moonlit beach. Hadn't forsaken all others for me. Hadn't even kissed me yet.

I sat up.

"What?" he asked, looking up at me with wide eyes, so like the embarrassed boy caught staring in the doorway. I tried to speak, to ask if he had done this with other girls, if he thought I had been with other boys, and if it mattered as much to him as it did to me. But I said nothing.

The raft lurched as he rolled to his feet. It was cold in his shadow. Even as I ordered myself to stand, to speak, to move even one finger, he jumped off the raft.

Hannah ran down the beach, the inner tube bouncing behind her on the sand. She closed her eyes and hopped over the sea foam. She waded to her ankles, then her knees. Her thighs were pink with cold. The giraffe floated beside her.

I welcomed the yawning sea, the weight of water on all sides, pressing against my mouth. I sensed the Undertoad crouched at the bottom, watching for my shadow to pass above him. As he wormed closer, his body rippling with anticipation, I dared him to catch my ankle and drag me down. His webbed fingers twitched toward my toes. Seaweed slid around my thighs as the Undertoad drew closer. My heart beat between my legs. Just within hooking distance, he retracted his long fingers and sank back into the deep. He no longer wanted me.

My feet scraped the slope, and I broke the surface. Hannah was thrashing back to the beach.

"The Undertoad took him!" she cried, as the giraffe bobbed away on the waves.

It was just David, tormenting her as he had tormented me.

But then he called out from behind me, "Don't be a baby."

Hannah stopped crying, as if slapped. Hurt jumped in her eyes. She stood on the beach, her knees red. The rain pushed across the ocean, shattering the waves into slivers around David, standing chest-deep among them.

"She's not a baby," I said, breaking the silence that had built up like silt over the summers. My voice came out too shrill, but I didn't care. "It's your fault she's scared." I let the words come, faster and sharper. "You were scared once, too."

He glared at me from the space between the shallows and the deep, and that's when I saw it: "You're still scared."

"I am not." His eyes were blue and accusing. "I'll get it, but then you'll owe me."

The sun glinted off his hair as he began to swim toward the giraffe, his shoulder blades rising and falling like wings. My stomach ached, hollowing out as if a line that had connected us was spinning out and out and out. The waves tugged at my waist, herding me to shore.

"The Undertoad took him, I saw," Hannah said, shivering on the beach.

I wrapped my towel around her shoulders as the rain met the beach, and she pressed against my side. I wanted to confess, to explain that I wasn't like the other girls. I felt everything more deeply. I felt with my nerves and the hairs on my arms. I felt my heart straining against my skin. I wanted handholding and roses and a film-finale kiss—but I also wanted David's palm sliding around my hip, and his tongue tracing my collarbone, and his fingers slipping inside my bathing suit.

"The Undertoad isn't real," I said.

David passed the raft, farther than any of us had ever gone, out where the waves were razors. His hair gleamed against the gray sky. The giraffe smiled back at him with painted lips, always just ahead. Again and again, David's fingers slipped off the rubber. Hannah began to cry.

Rain darkened the raft and steamed up the sand. The giraffe was just a speck in the distance. I could no longer see David. I took Hannah's hand.

The giraffe dipped out of sight and emerged again like a magician's trick. There was a flash of gold—David's hair—no, just one last gasp of sun on the waves. My heartbeat thrummed in new places. And the taste of salt, everywhere.

SIX ROSES

Rachel kissed her cousin last night. They were watching TV when he leaned across the couch and pressed his lips below her right earlobe. She jumped and turned so fast their lips touched. It only lasted a few seconds, and then he shifted away. She couldn't breathe. It was her first kiss.

She glances at the door, but it's safe in Liz's garage, where the four of us press knee to knee on the pool table. When she's nervous, Rachel winds the short curl at her temple around her finger.

"He used his tongue," she whispers, as if confessing. Her eyelashes are dark and wet.

"Cousins don't count," Liz says. And just like that, we're equals again.

Liz reaches across the stained felt of the pool table for another slice of pizza, and the slip she wears as a nightgown slides along her thighs. It's pink silk with lace straps. We covet that slip almost as much as we covet her brother, a senior who doesn't notice us, even though we sleep over every Saturday night. Amber says he notices her sometimes, when she's wearing a low-cut shirt. June says we can do better. She thinks she's so sophisticated, for someone who wears farm animal pajamas.

June's holding out for a man like Heathcliff or Mr. Darcy, whose scorn masks a deep pain only she can heal. She wants a kiss that will stop the earth from spinning, with a man who would die for her. If they were stranded in the ocean with only one plank of driftwood between them, he would insist she take it, and comfort her as he froze to death. No eighth-grader can compete with that. Nathan Bagley never stood a chance.

On the first day of summer, Nathan stood at the end of June's driveway for a full hour. Liz lives across the street, and she watched from the garage window while he leaned against his bike, chewing his thumbnail.

Every so often, he got on his bike and started down the driveway. When he reached the honeysuckle bushes, he turned back and stood there some more. When it was almost dark, he got on his bike again and, this time, sped straight down the middle of the driveway like he had a tornado at his back.

June's mother called up the stairs that she had a visitor. June came to the door, where Nathan stood on the other side of the screen. June had never spoken to him, though he'd been at our school since fifth grade, at least.

"Hi," he said.

"Hi," she said.

"Can you come out?"

He stood next to his bike in the driveway, and she stood on the top step.

"I wanted to ask you . . ." He stopped and looked up at her. He had sweat stains under his arms and his hair was sticking to his forehead. "Wannaseeamovietonight?"

"Oh, I can't," she said. "I have—"

Before she could come up with an excuse, he flipped his kickstand.

"Don't worry about it. Just thought I'd ask."

"Thank you," she said.

He didn't come back the next day, or the next, and it seemed that was that. June said she was relieved and a little sad to have hurt his feelings—but mostly relieved.

Any one of us would have gone to the movies with him. He's not handsome, like Liz's brother, but he's not so bad. None of that matters to June. She's such a snob she even thinks she's too good for us, sometimes.

Nathan showed up on June's doorstep again the next Sunday. This time, he did not ask her to the movies. He just asked if she'd liked *Frankenstein*, and she said she had, and he said he wished she'd been in his English class, because he was the only one who'd liked it. She asked what he'd liked about it, and came down all the porch steps, and they stood talking for a little while in the driveway.

He came back the next Sunday, and the next. They talked in the driveway, and soon they sat together on the steps. He did not mention movies or stare at her lips or touch her arm. He did none of the things Liz says boys do when they like you, and so June thought it would be safe to be his friend. We told her it's impossible to be just friends with boys, but she didn't listen.

Nathan taught her to ride a skateboard. They exchanged their favorite books. She introduced him to Jane Austen. He shared Stephen King. They played Game Boy under the magnolia tree. They talked while walking in circles around her yard. He was always so earnest. He made her feel like a difficult book, or a marble statue, or a landscape. She never invited him inside.

"Don't take him to your room," her mother warned her. "He'll tell everyone he saw your bed and ruin your reputation."

When June's mother was a girl, the preacher's son told everyone at school that he had slept with her. They believed him, because he was the preacher's son. June didn't think Nathan intended to ruin her reputation, but she was careful not to give him the opportunity.

He never invited her to his house. Amber thought maybe

he was embarrassed. She lives down the street from Nathan, whose house has dingy curtains and a sagging porch. She's heard a man's voice shouting inside. She's seen Nathan's mother rush outside in her nightgown (cotton, not silk) to kiss him goodbye at the bus stop. He'd kissed her back, even though Brian Whitehead made fun of him all the way to school.

One day, he gave June a bracelet of woven leather he'd made himself. His fingers were shaking as he tied it around her wrist. After he went home, she hid it on the top shelf of her closet under *Your Body, Your Treasure*, a book her mother had given her instead of "the talk."

"What's the matter? You want diamonds?" Liz asked.

"I don't want anything," June said. The next time Nathan came over, he didn't mention the bracelet. June said she had to accompany her mother to the library. They got into the car with their book bag, and Nathan escorted them down the driveway on his bike. He stopped at the end and watched them drive down the hill.

The library was closed. June and her mother waited in the parking lot for half an hour, listening to the radio. She felt bad about lying, but it was better than encouraging him, her mother said. When they got home with their empty bag, Nathan was gone.

The next time he knocked at the door, June said they were on their way to the library.

"Stop being a snob and go out with him," Liz said. He might

not have been the mysterious man June was waiting for, but at least he was nice.

She said she *knew* he was nice, and that's why she was lying to him. She didn't want him to like her *that* way, but she didn't want him to stop liking her, either.

"You're a tease," Liz said.

Yes, we agreed, she was a tease. Even in sheep pajamas, with a worried frown.

She avoided Nathan for a week—until one day he came to the door with six roses wrapped in cellophane. They crackled when he handed them to her, and the cellophane was slippery from his sweaty palms. She thanked him, but her knees were shaking. He was watching her, waiting for something else. Something more. She couldn't breathe. The roses crumpled in her fist.

"I like you, June," he said.

She wanted to sit down and run away at the same time. She wanted her mother to intervene. But the kitchen was empty behind her.

"I like you too," she said, but before he could say anything, just as the corners of his mouth began to lift, she darted in to add, "I like you as a friend."

Something in his eyes folded.

"Okay," he said, and shrugged. It was more of a twitch. "Happy birthday."

He reached out. To take the flowers back, she thought for a second. But no, he patted her shoulder, then swung his leg over his bike and wobbled away. That was the last time she saw him all summer.

"You're such a bitch," Liz said, and laughed.

"I am not." June's eyes filled with tears.

"You should have thanked him right."

She didn't elaborate, but we all knew what she meant.

"But I don't like him that way."

"So what?" Liz said.

It doesn't matter if you like a boy or not; it only matters if he likes *you*. Like Stan, who works at the CVS. He likes Amber, so she flirts with him in exchange for cigarettes. Last week, she finally let him kiss her. She said it wasn't so bad.

Stan is working tonight, so Amber goes behind the counter while we pocket lipstick, nail polish, blush. Even if Stan found out, he wouldn't tell, but June refuses to take the lipstick Liz presses into her hand. June could afford makeup, if she wanted it, but she has perfect skin like in the magazines, and she never steals. Liz slips it into her own pocket.

It's starting to rain, so we run back across the street to the hotel, where Liz's parents have rented a room for her birthday. The hotel is next to an overpass. Under the overpass, the bridge rats are smoking up. They watch us run by, their eyes blurred under their hoods. We wave, they wave back, but

June turns up the collar of her raincoat and pretends not to see them.

The lobby is empty. A streak of wet footprints on the tile floor is the only sign that there's anyone else here. The furniture is pretty shabby, and the elevator creaks, and our room smells like stale cigarettes. But we don't mention any of that to Liz. It's still a great birthday party, even if her parents are in the adjoining room.

We spread the makeup on the desk and Liz sits on the bed. Her hair frizzes at the temples. We conceal the acne on her forehead, give her cheeks some color, and fill in her eyebrows, which she's plucked too thin. She's too impatient to let them grow back. She's impatient with her nails, too, and bites them down to nubs. She paints them to hide their ragged edges. As the polish chips, she just glosses over them again until they're lumpy, like a wall that's been painted too many times. We strip her nails and paint them pale pink to match her slip.

We give Amber's dumpling face some angles and part Rachel's hair on the right to hide her widow's peak. June won't let us pluck her unibrow. She says that's the way her eyebrows grow, and she doesn't see any reason to change it. She doesn't wear makeup, either, but it's Liz's birthday, so she sits on the edge of the bed. Her knobby knees stick out from the hem of her shorts. Her legs are goose pimpled, and each hairless pore stands up, red with razor burn.

"Did you shave your legs with a butter knife again?" Liz asks.

June's fingers twitch over her knees and interlace in her lap. Sometimes, we say things just to see what she'll do.

Liz pulls up the desk chair so their faces are level. She flicks powder across June's cheeks and forehead. She spikes June's eyelashes and slashes her lips with "Tramp" red and bruises her eyelids. When we turn June to the mirror, her face goes still. She looks away from her reflection.

We walk through the lobby in our bathing suits, but there's no one to impress except each other. In the hot tub, the makeup streaks down our faces and drips from our chins. We dunk our heads and emerge clean and red. We lean back against the jets, and the vibration makes our breasts bounce.

"Hey June," Amber says, arching back against the jets. "Do you know what 'sixty-nine' means?"

June sinks in the heaving water and pretends not to hear.

"She doesn't know!" Liz shrieks.

She never knows. We had to explain sex in fourth grade. She says "genitals" like our science textbook. Once, we asked if she wanted to join the PEN-15 club, and she let us write PEN15 on the back of her hand. When she realized what it spelled, she didn't talk to us for the rest of the day. She'd thought it was real, like the Babysitters Club.

Voices echo from the locker room, and five boys burst through the glass doors and hurtle into the pool, their bodies swift and dark like seals beneath the surface.

"They're probably from Linton," Rachel whispers. They must be. We know all the boys in Westfield.

They heave up out of the pool, their arm muscles straining, and vault into the hot tub. Water sloshes onto the floor. We scream, pretending to be afraid. They crush between us, and we press back against the jets. A boy with a diamond stud earring slings his arm over June's shoulder. It's his birthday, he says. They have a room upstairs, too. June sinks up to her chin. Her cheeks are flushed, and her eyelashes are so thick, even without mascara.

A boy with a faint mustache runs his hand up Amber's arm, dangerously close to the trim of her bikini top. His hand is big and dark against her skin.

When we're fainty-hot, we emerge from the hot tub. The mustached boy holds a towel open for Amber like a fur coat. We follow them out to the parking lot, where we sit on the front steps. Three boys cram among us on the steps and the other two strut off across the parking lot.

"What are we doing?" June asks. She'd rather be upstairs watching a movie, like Liz's parents.

"Hanging out," Liz says, lighting a cigarette.

She shares her cigarette with the mustached boy. She has reapplied her lipstick, and the tip of the cigarette is stained red, but he doesn't seem to mind. The others pull up in a dented Buick, and the boy who shares Liz's cigarette puts his arm around her and says, "You wanna come?"

She plucks the cigarette from his mouth and takes a drag, studying the car while he studies her. She stands, brushing off her thighs.

"You can't!" June jumps off the step, gripping her towel around her chest so tight it bites into her armpits.

"Why not?" Liz turns to her, waiting for something more, as if she really wants a reason.

"You don't know them," June says.

"So what?" Liz says, and slides into the back seat, followed by the boy with the mustache. He shuts the door. The others lounge on the steps, leaning back on their elbows.

"Don't worry," says the one with the earring. "He'll take care of her."

We watch the car pull away. Liz waves through the back window, and when she's gone, it's quiet. Amber and Rachel pass a cigarette back and forth. June just stands at the bottom of the stairs with her towel clamped around her chest. It's dark, and the parking lot is nearly empty. We can hear each other breathing. One of the boys is peeling a splinter off the porch railing.

"You wanna come up?" he asks, without looking at us.

June just stares at the empty road.

"We would," Amber says, "but we'll wait for our friend." He shrugs and grinds out his cigarette, almost in relief.

"Room 202, if you change your mind," he says as they disappear into the lobby.

We won't change our minds. The street is empty and quiet.

"What if her parents ask where she is?" Rachel curls her hair around and around her finger.

"We'll tell them she's in the bathroom," Amber says.

"We can't lie." June's eyes glitter with tears. "We have to tell. We have to—"

"She would kill us," Amber says. "Let's go back upstairs. If her parents ask, we'll say she's at the vending machine."

June starts to cry in the elevator.

"That's not helping," Amber says.

But June can't stop. She huddles on the bed with her face to the wall. Amber pulls the desk chair to the window and looks down at the parking lot. The window will only open a crack, but there's nothing to hear anyway. Rachel sits beside June. She pats her back, but June doesn't move, so she turns on the TV.

"What if something happens to her?" Rachel whispers to Amber. "What if—"

"Shut up," Amber says.

The shadows of the bridge rats are moving below the overpass. A light flicks on under the adjoining door of Liz's parents' room. We hold our breath. The toilet flushes on the other side of the wall. June curls tighter on the bed. The sliver of light under the door goes out again, and Amber closes her eyes. Her stomach hurts. Rachel climbs under the covers, pressing her side against June's. She tries to watch music videos, but her mind slips around the songs.

We blink in and out of sleep. The music videos are over and a dating show begins. Amber shuts off the TV.

"Okay . . ." she says, as if making up her mind about something, but leaves the thought unfinished.

A car door slams below. Amber sits on the other bed and flips open a magazine. We wait for the clanging of the elevator, not quite believing we'll hear it. And we don't.

Liz opens the door. She's run up the stairs.

Breathless, she strips off her bathing suit, whispering about the boy, and the car ride, and his hands and lips. The tender skin under her nose is raw from his faint mustache. She changes into her silk nightgown and curls her legs beneath her on the bed next to Amber. He'd kissed her, and it was just like she'd imagined. As she talks, she picks the paint from her nails. It flakes onto the bedspread.

◆ ◆ ◆

Something has changed. It's not just that we haven't seen June for a few days, and she won't answer the phone. It's more than that, a sense of unraveling. We press together knee to knee.

Liz says she doesn't notice a thing, as she paints a coat of blue polish over the chipped pink. The smell fills the garage, and Rachel jumps down from the pool table to open the window. She calls us over to look across the street.

Nathan Bagley is riding his bike up June's driveway. He rides slow and steady. He rides with purpose.

"Doesn't he ever quit?" Liz asks without looking up and starts painting her toenails.

Nathan disappears around the honeysuckle bushes.

Now, he'll get off his bike and flip up his kickstand. He'll knock on June's door. She will not go to the library today. She will open the door, and she will be glad to see him. She'll barely notice the sweat rings under his arms.

"Hi," June will say.

They'll walk into the yard, and she will be aware of him beside her, aware of his quick breathing and the way he keeps sneaking glances at her. She'll pretend not to notice. Her hands will shake, and she'll hide them in the pockets of her shorts.

He'll talk about his paper route and describe the plot of *The Stand*. He'll ask if she had a good summer, and if she's ready to start high school. June will admit she's nervous, even though she's smart and works hard and gets straight As. It's just that she feels like everything's changing, and she's not sure she wants things to change quite so much. Not yet.

Nathan will say he understands what she means. He's nervous, too. And the way he'll say it, gentle and serious, will make her look up at him. He's nice, and he likes so many of the same things she does, and he likes *her.*

They'll walk slowly in silence, like you do in museums. She'll think maybe she can see him clearly now. And she'll begin to see herself clearly, too. She's too careful, with her childish pajamas and buttoned-up shirts. She has bushy eyebrows and a pimple near her right ear. She doesn't want the boys who want her, but she wants them to want her.

Who is she to turn down a nice guy like Nathan? Who is she to expect romance and fireworks and a man who would die for her? Who the hell does she think she is? Six roses should be enough.

They'll end up at the edge of the driveway where he parked his bike. When they stop walking, the silence will change. He'll rest his palm on the seat, patting it like a horse. He'll look up at the treetops and down at the gravel and anywhere but at her.

"Thank you for coming," she'll say. Her voice will fill her head like it does right before you pass out. She'll long for the safety of the garage, to be pressed knee to knee with us again.

"Well," he'll say.

"Well."

His hand will drop from the bike seat, and he'll step toward her, his breathing getting faster. He will pull her close, pinning her left arm to her side. She'll pat his shoulder blade, and his back will be damp.

He'll press his lips just below her right earlobe. She'll hope he won't notice her pimple as his lips slide to her cheek. Everything will seem too loud and bright as his mouth meets the corner of hers. She'll turn her head a fraction of an inch.

His lips will be soft, but his faint mustache will scrape the skin under her nose. She won't know what to do with her hands. His lips will part a little and hers, too, and he'll tilt his head and breathe into her mouth, and there will be no fireworks, and the earth will not stop spinning, but it won't be so bad.

DESIREE THE DESTROYER

Eve's doctor recommends she draw a map of her breasts to become familiar with their topography. Eve imagines such a map, veined with blue-green rivers, the ridge of her breastbone—a mysterious world she never wants to visit.

Desiree the Destroyer's breasts overflow her spandex jumpsuit, and she dusts them with glitter so they catch the cage lights. She knows how to make an impression. Her spiked kneepads leave puncture wounds in her competitors' thighs. Her mother sews her costumes with liberal use of sequins. Desiree the Destroyer designs her own capes.

When Eve was growing up, her mother sewed her clothes from ten-cent pattern books. Their covers depicted girls in ruffled dresses. In middle school, the other kids teased Eve, but she couldn't tell her mother she wanted clothes from the mall. Eve is thirty, and her mother still makes her dresses.

At thirty, Desiree the Destroyer still lives with her mother, who lures practice partners into the garage with milk and cookies. The pesticide-sprayer from next door, the throat-clearer from across the street, the drag-racer from down the block. As the door slides shut behind them, they blink in confusion. Cookies crumble in their fists. Desiree the Destroyer strides down the stairs from the mudroom, her cape billowing, her décolletage glittering. They freeze in wonder before her.

There was the creep who parked his van across from the elementary school. Desiree the Destroyer crushed his groin. There was the paperboy who lobbed the Sunday edition through her mother's sun porch window. Desiree the Destroyer planted her knee on his neck and made him weep for mercy. There was the Doberman that terrorized small children. Desiree the Destroyer tore out its throat.

Eve is a champion of the English language. She arranges her office supplies parallel to the edges of the desk and does not initiate conversation with the other proofreader, Nancy, who shares her cubicle. Nancy is the type of woman Eve could easily become, if she were less vigilant. Nancy signs her emails "Thx." She wears low-cut shirts that reveal her collarbones. She uses both drink tickets at the company holiday party. Nancy has an online dating profile.

Still, Eve is eager to appear friendly. She knows everyone's birthday and favorite donut. She approaches office relationships with the same precision she devotes to tracking her time. (Break for water: one minute, forty-seven seconds.) Her boss has suggested she is perhaps too diligent, though he appreciates her attention to detail. When she tries to ease up, her attention to detail drags her back into thoroughness. Eve fears she is a car with blown-out brakes sliding down a hill. No one is looking. She slips her fingers into her shirt.

When Desiree the Destroyer got her first period, she and her mother made cave paintings on the walls with her menstrual blood. Now, she flaunts her buoyant breasts and lets her leg hair grow long and sleek. Her thighs glisten like a thoroughbred's. At the farmer's market, she lets old women pile vegetables on her back and makes deliveries to their houses for pocket change.

Eve informed her boss about the doctor's appointment a week ago, but she reminds him in an email now, lest he should think she is taking a long lunch. Her computer clock clicks toward noon. Couldn't she sneak out a few minutes early?

Her boss isn't even in his office. He wouldn't know if she left at 11:52 p.m—but *she* would know.

Desiree the Destroyer can crush a skull between her thighs. Sometimes, she squeezes just enough to make a competitor pass out. Some men like that.

Every Monday at nine, Eve watches cage fighting. She treats herself to low-cal popcorn and takes notes in a dedicated spiral-bound notebook.

Desiree the Destroyer grips the chain link enclosure and throws her head back as the spectators' screams throb through her body. They love it, but she doesn't do it for them. She is in thrall to her desires. This is what makes her such a successful sexual partner. Desiree the Destroyer wears her cape to bed, and she is always on top.

Eve hates when people tell her to smile. She concentrates so hard on appearing pleasant that she often forgets to breathe. Last year, she nearly passed out at the company holiday party hosted by the bowling alley. Eve doesn't begrudge her colleagues the opportunity to bowl, but the choice of venue excludes her from bonding with them. Bowling shoes cause athlete's foot, gangrene, and foot odor, and ball finger holds are breeding grounds for bacteria. Eve knows certain people don't wash their hands, despite the sign she hung above the sink in the ladies' room.

Desiree the Destroyer thrusts her thumbs into Somerset Sparkles's eye sockets and roars.

At noon, Eve notes noon in her timekeeping notebook, followed by "Lunch appointment," and gathers her things. In the hall, she passes a cluster of buckets catching rainwater. Her blouse sticks to her back. Her stockings are sweating.

Desiree the Destroyer grips her opponents by the ponytail and mops the mat with their faces. She shaves her head so her opponents won't have anything to hold onto.

Eve clutches the rape whistle on her keychain as she enters the parking garage. She wonders if the lot attendants will think she is sneaking out early, or that she is so privileged she can come and go as she pleases. "No! I'm just like you," she wants to assure them. Except she is not. She works in an air-conditioned office, while they sit in a box all day getting rained on every time they slide back the ticket window.

Desiree the Destroyer loves the stink of the ring. Even when freshly mopped, the mat retains the tang of blood. The ancient Romans didn't mop the Coliseum. She ignores the spectators who waddle in, arms full of beer and nachos, to fill the seats around the chain link fence. She hates to hear them chewing as she fights. When Desiree the Destroyer bleeds, she flings her blood into the stands.

Eve's skin is greenish in the fluorescent lights of the doctor's office. Her knees stick out from under her paper gown, sharp like trowels. Last time, she thought she might have spine cancer, but it was just mild arthritis. Her writing arm is wearing down. She is an aggressive proofreader.

On the back of the door, there is a poster illustrating proper hand washing technique. Eve's cleanliness makes her feel superior, though she is ashamed of feeling superior. She does not believe in pride. But when she's right, she has a responsibility to share her knowledge with others.

Last week, Eve wrote a letter to Clifford Meathammer, who had been her favorite actor until he was photographed leaving a club with yet another model. It was time he settled down, she wrote, and stopped objectifying women. Besides, models don't make good mothers. They're too thin to provide welcoming wombs.

Desiree the Destroyer is disgusted by children, whose bodies are like those boneless fish lurking in the deep sea. She does not have mothering instincts; the deficiency only heightens her other senses. Desiree the Destroyer can anticipate a punch by the slightest shift of her opponent's torso and deflect a kick with the grace of a cougar. She is constantly alert. She can't afford to let her guard down. That's how she lost her front teeth. Now, she wears false ones that snap in and out.

The doctor knocks and opens the door. Doctors never wait for an invitation. Eve pulls the gown tight across her chest. What happened to matronly Doctor Fleischer, with her plain face and shapeless dresses? Doctor Fleischer isn't impatient or scolding, but leans against the sink and listens to Eve's list of symptoms and speculative diagnosis. "What did I tell you about WebMD?" she asks, as if it's their private joke. She smooths the wax paper invitingly and warms her fingers under the faucet. This doctor does not warm his fingers. He is young and has eyes like a Scottish loch she saw in a travel book. He instructs Eve to lie down.

Desiree the Destroyer struts under the cage lights. The lights cook the sequins on her jumpsuit, and when the flesh of her inner arm brushes against them, they sting. The chain link burns her shoulder blades. Someday, she'll travel the world in a glittering cape sewn from an American flag. Desiree the Destroyer has never been anywhere. She is hungry for an expanded worldview.

Eve's nipples stand up in the clinical air. She averts her eyes as the doctor presses the pads of his fingers into her right breast. He kneads under her armpit, working his way in. Eve watches his serene face for a flicker of worry. He squeezes her nipple. The pain is dull and pleasant. She wishes he would squeeze harder.

The challenger stretches on the opposite side of the cage. Scrappy Sue's jumpsuit has ruffles, and her thinness reeks of self-deprivation. Her arms are like chicken wings. When Desiree the Destroyer eats chicken wings, she digs her fingers between the bones and pops out the meat. She eyes Scrappy's arm flesh. Maybe the spectators would enjoy a bite or two. A little blood between her teeth.

Once, in college, a boy liked Eve back. She couldn't speak around him, could barely look into his eyes, which were the blue-gray of a calm ocean that held its own light. She tried to meet his eyes in glimpses, to show she was paying attention. He talked about himself at length, which she appreciated because it meant she didn't have to speak.

When he ended things with his girlfriend and asked Eve to accompany him to the museum, she was deeply unsettled by the way her fantasy life had begun to merge with reality. He took her to the instrument room and, standing close behind her, conducted the brass section with an unlit cigarette. She stared at their reflection in a tuba and tried to determine what he liked about her.

Scrappy Sue is all chicken bones and gristle. Her eyes dart around the ring, and Desiree the Destroyer cackles in the face of such bald fear. The satisfying thwack of her foot against Scrappy's cheek reverberates through her flanks. Her sequins burn. She'll mop the ring with Scrappy's ponytail and season the spectators' nachos with her blood.

His roommate called Eve his "girlfriend, or whatever," and she wondered if that's what she was. The question was never resolved. Not when he put his arm around her at the movies. Not when he tapped out Mozart's Requiem on her knee. Not when he finally kissed her on his unmade bed. She was stunned by the thickness of his tongue, by her own eagerness, and by the question that leapt unbidden into her head: "Is this all?"

Scrappy darts in with a shovel shot to the liver. Desiree the Destroyer's legs go numb and she staggers gasping against the chains.

The shelf above his bed still displayed three framed photos of his former girlfriend, from which Eve averted her eyes. She should have asked him to take the photos down, but she was careful not to be a shrewish girlfriend—if she was in fact his girlfriend. She still wasn't sure, even as his hands skimmed up her sides, her stomach, until she gently, but firmly, took them away. She tried to slow her heart, to breathe in time with his probing tongue. He told her she had too many restrictions. His hands scrabbled in her palms like birds.

When he ended it, he said, "I need more in a relationship," and Eve realized it had been a relationship, after all. He was a little drunk. She avoided his bleary eyes as he helped her into her coat. She refused his offer to walk her home. Alone on the sidewalk, she struggled to breathe, thinking maybe she'd loved him.

Lying in the doctor's office with her breasts exposed, she feels as she did then, in the expectant silence of his bedroom under the gaze of his former girlfriend. This remains her most erotic memory. It often returns to her in the dark.

Desiree the Destroyer might really be dying this time. The spectators' chewing is so goddamn loud.

The doctor doesn't feel anything out of the ordinary, he says. As a precaution, he sends Eve down the hall, where a nurse mashes the tender mass of veins and capillaries between two panes. Eve turns her head away, but she imagines her breast like a jellyfish flushed up on the sand, clear and liverlike, with its tendrils crushed beneath it. She can barely look at herself in the shower.

Desiree the Destroyer has trained her organs to absorb direct impact by sprinting through the car wash. She orders herself to pull it together; her mother didn't sew this costume for her to die in. She deflects a jab to the solar plexus, and counters with a left hook to the chin that sends Scrappy spinning. Scrappy scrambles to reset her fighting stance. Her legs are so skinny she could fit a cantaloupe in the gap between her thighs. A layer of ruffles obscures her breasts.

Desiree the Destroyer tugs her neckline down. She'd had a ponytail once, and teeth. She'd claimed to be holding back so she wouldn't hurt anyone. So *she* wouldn't get hurt again. What a chickenshit virgin, all technical proficiency and no heart. What a liar. What a waste! She rears up to her full glittering height and flips Scrappy ass over heels.

By the time the results come back clear, Eve has gnawed her lip raw and made tentative peace with her mortality. She's outlined her remaining time on earth: she'd quit her job and blow her savings on a trip to Scotland. She'd eat whatever she wanted and shop at the mall. She'd have sex. She'd get drunk just once, to see what it felt like to lose control.

Scrappy clings to Desiree the Destroyer's back, digging her heels into her gut. The spectators scream, and Desiree the Destroyer snaps her head back into Scrappy's nose. Her neck turns warm and wet. She pins Scrappy beneath her knee, squashing her cheek against the mat. One eye rolls up to peer at Desiree the Destroyer, reminding her of a flounder. It doesn't make Desiree the Destroyer feel powerful. It just makes her sad. This moment always does.

The spectators' screams have crested. If she doesn't end it, they will leave her kneeling in silence. She drives her forehead into Scrappy's. Slides her teeth along Scrappy's neck and clamps onto the soft flesh below her ear. She shakes her head like a lion and tears free, restored by the taste of blood.

Eve is usually ashamed when dressing in a room that's not her own, but she does not indulge the shame today. She has cheated death again.

The announcer buckles the championship belt around Desiree the Destroyer's waist. She allows his fingers to graze her ass cheek as he cinches it tight. The belt hugs her hips like a strong lover, though Desiree the Destroyer is hard-pressed to find a lover whose strength rivals her own. Her cape billows in the breeze of the spectators' screams, but she does not hear them. She raises her hot face to the cage lights.

As Eve emerges into the sun, she waits for the relief that lowers the tenuous boundary between life and death, allowing her to appreciate the fragility of human existence and the fact that she's alive. She smiles, splitting open her gnawed lip. With the taste of blood in her mouth, she stuffs her stockings into her purse and unlocks her car. She doesn't have to go back to work just yet.

Desiree the Destroyer lets loose on the open highway, kicking the gas until the six-cylinder engine roars. She unbuckles her championship belt so she can breathe.

CRUSH

At the company party, the pregnant wives give me knowing looks. They pass gas and wisdom, boast of swollen ankles, tender breasts and burst blood vessels—sufferings blissfully borne. One sets her sparkling water on the shelf of her stomach and says, "Last night, the baby turned, and I could feel its spine." I shudder and sip my beer. I'd be afraid to roll in sleep and crush its vertebrae, slight like a stuffed sparrow, bones held in place by thread and glue. Afraid to crush, but tempted, too.

FORESIGHT

Foresight arrives in an Amazon box. Susan thinks of the man she has stopped loving and the job she hates. She is tired of life lessons. They bring her no closer to figuring out what she wants. Foresight tastes like liquid cotton candy. She lies back on the couch with her eyes closed.

She will remain on the couch, waiting. Her waiting will curdle until she forgets what she was waiting for. She will develop bedsores. She will line up soap operas so there's no time to question her choices. A mouse will die in the wall and she will not bother to find it. The house will fill with the sweet stink of its decay, indistinguishable from the stink of her own body. Her teeth will rot, she will cultivate a yeast infection, and mold will grow under her arms. Her ass crack will fill with fur. She will become one with the couch.

No—she will rise. She will get dressed and have lunch downtown and attend an author reading. When the balding author signs her book, she will be daring and invite him to coffee. He will say yes because he is poor and thirsty, and she is still pretty. They will go around the corner to a nondescript coffee shop that will become "their place." When they move to the middle of nowhere for the only teaching position he can get, they will remember that coffee shop with nostalgia. She will live in the idyllic past, which will become a source of friction between them. They will alleviate the friction by having first one child and then another. She will mourn who she could have been, while struggling to appreciate the life she has. And when he cheats on her with a student, she will wish she were dead.

She will not go to the author reading. She will walk past the bookstore, averting her gaze from the man at the podium. She will take the train to Newbury Street, where she will simply stroll and window shop. She'll buy herself a necklace to remember this day, her narrow escape. But this day will have no bearing on the rest of her life. She will forget where she bought the necklace and give it to the daughter she'll have with the man she will meet online. She will initiate contact with the man she knows will treat her best, who won't cheat or lie. Some of the others would be better lovers, would take her on trips, worship her, kill for her—but this one will be kind and loyal and give her a beautiful daughter who won't die like the one she'd have with the musician or turn to drugs like the banker's son. Or become boring and sullen, like the philosopher's daughter who would visit only on Christmas.

She is amazed by how similar her children would look, and yet how different. Their fathers' DNA lengthens and shortens their faces, widens and narrows their eyes, rounds their chins, punches dimples in their cheeks. She will be a different mother to each; comforting to the doctor's son who strives for approval, strict to the chef's daughter whose caginess is all too familiar. She will be a different wife, too. She will care for the gentle man when he is dying of prostate cancer, though she has been cuckolding him for years. She will abandon the teacher and their son to travel the world, but will only get as far as Albuquerque. She will take her daughters screaming from the IT guy.

She will be a writer, a real estate agent, a small shop owner; she will celebrate Christmas at a full table, or by watching the Charlie Brown special with mice in the walls and moss in her ears. In none of her lives will she be brilliant or famous or content. Her mediocrity will hound her through a kaleidoscope of futures. She will try to select the one that holds the least pain. But every time she commits to a path, a new choice splits it into still more paths, until she reaches the end and there are no choices left to make.

All the possible futures branch and collapse in front of her. She will stand in the middle of the sidewalk until the dizziness passes. She will turn right or left or throw herself before a bus or just stand here until someone pushes her from behind. She will take Foresight again tomorrow, or she will flush it, preferring the unknown. Or, she will order a year's supply. Until she decides, she will stand here, and stand, and stand.

THE VANISHING POINT

Diana puts on the deer head when she gets home from work. She's constructed the steel frame to rest comfortably on her shoulders. The felted aluminum plates lend her face the contours of an airplane hangar. At first, the snout tubes were uncomfortable, but her nostrils have toughened. She gives Jehovah's Witnesses a shock.

She'd toyed with the idea of moving to Canada—but she'd done the moving-for-a-new-life thing before. New places quickly become old, as do clothes, habits, and men. She always returns to herself. Diana needs a change she can't come back from.

She's modeled the head on a vision that keeps her up at night, one she pulls tight around herself as she sits in rush-hour traffic. She longs for silence.

The vision burrows into her and spreads as she eats lunch at her desk, as she revises a research paper she'd hoped would help earn her tenure, as she locks her biomechanics lab for the night. She sinks into the deep velvet woods.

The fawn had appeared in the untamed field behind her childhood home. He'd grazed in the shade of the magnolia tree, one hind leg pulled up in pain. As the fawn had tripped after his mother, Diana and her father had mourned his certain death.

Their grief was premature. He returned the following spring, and though his wound had healed, he still hitched up his hind leg. As he grazed with his mother and sure-footed sisters, he bowed his muzzle, revealing the buds of antlers. He's a survivor, Diana's father said.

Diana studied the fawn through her father's binoculars, his flanks rippling as he shivered off flies, the white flash of his tail, the way his legs tucked up as he leapt the stone wall like an ocean wave. She watched him from her bedroom window.

The fawn, now a stag, returned every spring. His sisters started their own families and moved on. His mother stopped accompanying him.

Diana constructs a torso with materials she'd used to design a durable exosuit for soldiers. She builds outward, adapting her S-shaped spine to the deer's rolling curve. She sets the torso at an incline, repositioning the *foramen magnum*, the "great hole" through which the spine connects to the skull.

The frame relieves the stress four-legged motion exerts on her joints and enhances her muscle propulsion to rival a deer's. She runs bicycle brake cables down the lengths of her legs, tipped with steel hooves. She fabricates sensors for her eyelids to open and close her deer eyes.

She preps her gut for a deer's diet by boosting her roughage intake, swapping out Lean Cuisines for salads. After a week, she ditches the salad dressing. Then the croutons and nuts, and finally the bacon bits, until all that's left are greens. She mixes in some grass from the esplanade and shredded maple leaves with an aftertaste of decay.

Last year, she'd almost completed the kale and cauliflower diet—but this is worse. The leaves stick in her teeth. The grass bunches in her throat.

To enable digestion, she considered fecal transplants that would boost her microbiomes, but a consultation with a biologist yields a more elegant grazing method: She masticates the grass into a pulp, which she spits into a tube connected to an artificial stomach converted from a colonoscopy bag. There, the grass is broken down into a smoothie of volatile fatty acids and cultured microbes, which Diana consumes through a straw.

She still doesn't enjoy the taste of grass, though she's tried every local variety from the sweet lawn outside her lab to the nutty scruff along the I-93. She has become accustomed to the bitter hint of insecticide.

Diana studies YouTube videos to practice the deer dialogue of threatening snorts, jovial bleats, amorous wheezes. The stomp and pant of alarm and the white tail of retreat. She rigs her own tail with a pulley connected to her pointer finger so she can raise and lower it at will. To offset the suit's mechanical nature, she applies synthetic fur to every inch of hide.

She orders a vial of Stag Stink from a hunting catalogue. Bottled from hormones distilled from buck urine, it's guaranteed to mask human odors, allowing her to infiltrate a herd.

She'll have to stop showering eventually, but for now she's still a professional. The lab director intends for her to take over the department after he retires and has already outlined a ten-year-plan for the transition. Phil has been at the university for thirty-five years and is the last to leave every night. He steers every conversation to his latest research; currently, the neuromechanics of flamingo balance. It would be so easy to bide her time until Phil retires and slip into his office, and his habits.

Diana cuts back to two showers a week, then one. It becomes harder to invest in empty routines.

Her grad student Lou molds the suit to her specifications.

A chemist studying the composition of snail mucus, Lou 3D-prints prosthetics for wounded wildlife in his spare time. An eagle's beak, a dog's leg, a bat's wing. He prints plates of armored bone to fit over Diana's augmented musculature.

"It's kind of like Pups," he says, kneeling to take the measurements of her inseam for Nylon panels to prevent chafing. "You know, those guys who wear dog costumes? They eat off the floor, sleep in crates, play catch. They even have handlers. Sometimes they have sex."

"It's nothing like that," Diana says. "I don't like dogs—and there won't be any sex."

"Not a dog person," he says, as if cataloging this new fact about her.

In exchange for Lou's help and discretion, Diana had promised he could document her transformation and publish a paper upon her return.

"What does Kevin think of all this?" he asks, careful not to look at her while he records her measurements, his laptop balanced in the crook of his arm.

"It doesn't matter," she says.

Lou turns to her with the full force of his concern.

"I'll stop pestering you," he says. "Just promise to bring a phone for emergencies and give me a call every few days so I'll know you're alive, okay?"

"Fine," she says to shut him up. She would feel bad deceiving Lou, if he didn't already have it made. At just thirty, he'd arrived at MIT with a fellowship and a baby on the way, while Diana had to put her life on hold for postdoc after postdoc, sucking up to male researchers just for the chance to pursue her work.

Every time she got close to promotion, some fresh heartbreak had derailed her; she took a leave of absence when her mother was diagnosed with pancreatic cancer, and another to care for her aging father. Now she's finally an assistant professor, but she's got nothing else to show for her sacrifices. Lou doesn't need to know she's not coming back.

Diana stands four-legged in the alley between her apartment building and the neighbor's house, cultivating a deer's quiet mind. She'd studied meditation at the monastery in the strip mall. The teacher had instructed the class to pick something on which to fix their gaze and focus their *chi*.

She stares at her license plate, ignoring how silly she must look, the ache blooming in her lower back, the quaking of her arms and thighs. Something is digging into her palm. A shard of glass, maybe. It could slice her hand, injecting bacteria into her bloodstream. She can feel the bacteria pushing up into her wrist, her inner arm. Her veins are bulging. She is going to die of infection before she even leaves home.

She flexes one knee, then the other. Rolls her head, scraping her spine against the great hole.

The neighbor's shade is lopsided and her windows are

streaked with small handprints. Rain skates down Diana's neck. Kevin had wanted kids.

He'd described their hypothetical children as if to tempt her with their genetic superiority. Their aptitude for music and math, their curly hair, their predisposition for glasses and braces. She'd insisted again and again that she didn't want them, that she'd *never* wanted kids. He began heading to work earlier and coming home later. He brought little gifts and picked big fights, wearing her down until she stopped arguing. He'd taken her silence for consideration. That's what he said when he left her.

She'd never swayed in her conviction. *He's* the one who'd changed his mind—who said, early on, that he would be happy either way, as long as he spent his life with her. But she hadn't been enough for him. And that was the end of it, because she deserved to be enough for someone.

When he left, months ago, he'd stripped his belongings from their apartment—his grandparents' furniture and the framed blueprints of condos he'd designed, his flannel sheets, his pots and pans. He'd left the rooms practically bare. In the two years they'd lived together, Diana had never realized how few possessions she'd brought into their home.

She takes what's left to Goodwill—until she's cast off everything, along with Kevin and the person she'd been—and comes away with herself alone.

Diana leaves her car, with the keys in the ignition, at the end of the road whose name she occasionally writes on government documents by mistake. The crabapple trees guarding the mile-long driveway are overgrown and the house's trim is flaking. The porch boards are buckling. The bushes have blinded the kitchen windows.

For two years, she's been promising to put the house up for sale. Bracing herself to sort through her family's things, her old treasures still arranged in her bedroom like a memorial to her childhood. She used to come home just to sleep, to feel like herself again. She hasn't been home since her father died.

He had taught art and painted portraits on commission, and his home was as meticulous as his craft. He didn't make a mess, only a little dust that she vacuumed twice a week. When he was too frail to play tennis, as he had every Tuesday and Thursday, he followed her around the house straightening the paintings she disturbed with the duster. When he died, she didn't change a thing.

Diana dons the exosuit under the magnolia tree where as a girl she'd built a fort. Its soft-furred buds are folded tight.

Her hooves are designed to absorb the shock of her tread. Still, the impact hums up her shins, through her knees, up the highway of her back. She lingers at the boundary where field meets woods. The biologist had said deer live at the edges between worlds, along highways and in suburban backyards. As if they can't decide where they belong.

The air is crisp with pine and the vestiges of winter. Mt. Greylock is still capped with snow; the water it sheds into the creek behind the house is so pure she and her mother had used it to make lemonade.

Her hooves sink into the damp grass like high heels at an outdoor wedding. She pushes into the woods, tamping down her unease, the archaic dread of straying too far from home.

Her mother had forbidden her to pass the creek, where a swath of ground drops off into a trench. She'd dutifully remained in the shallow woods. As a teen, she'd rebelled by exploring along the creek—but had never crossed over.

How foolish, to still feel bound by that decades-old directive. But she feels the eyes of the house on her as she plunges into the creek, savoring the shock of water on her flanks. The creek invades the gaps between her bodies, dousing her human thighs. Her wet skin slaps against the insides of her deer-body's haunches.

The snout tubes condense the air into purified pine. The dying winter exhales wood smoke and musk. For the first time in years, Diana can fill her lungs. She hadn't realized how deprived of breath she'd become.

Diana breathes deeply, as she learned in meditation, relishing the silence, the separation of mind from matter. She sidles up to squirrels, a hesitant hedgehog, a clutch of rabbits who startle and flee. A chipmunk skitters to a stop before her and she extends a foreleg in greeting. It bolts, screeching, *Abomination!*

She loses sight of the house beyond the tangle of trees. It doesn't matter if she never finds her way back; the forest, in all its majesty and mystery, is her home now.

At first the woods seem quiet, but she soon finds that the silence is all her own, a symptom of her human shortcomings. The woods resound with the breath of trees. Leaves crashing into each other. The apelike shriek of the barred owl. And the air! She had never thought of it as alive. But it is joyously, calamitously alive. The wind strokes her flanks, buffets her ears, plays across her pelt. She is mesmerized by the catastrophic violence of the forest.

Here are remnants of the logging trail her great-grandfather and his horses had used to drag trees off the mountain and into town. Diana follows its ragged outline until it erases itself. She grazes below a stand of birches whose bark is stripped from branch to root. She scans the woods for her brethren, but there is no one. She savors the sour grit of stiff grass, grinding it between her molars and spitting the juices into the tube that runs into the digestive chamber. Her first meal in earnest. The grass gives her cramping gas, but there's no one to mind. She relishes her freedom from humiliation.

Diana is dismayed by how quickly she fatigues, despite her preparations. Her human shoulders and wrists ache from bearing her weight, and her hooves are already rubbing her heels raw. She tries to give herself over to deer-body and abolish the inadequate human one underneath.

The night brings relief. She's survived the first day. Her joints ache. Her bodies are so heavy she can barely stand. She turns in place, seeking direction. But she's lost.

She can't be lost, she tells herself; the forest is her home. She scours the impersonal trees for a sign that she hasn't made a terrible mistake, but they pull their shadows close. She turns in a clumsy circle, her legs rattling the joint bolts. She fumbles at her chinstrap, dizzy with mounting panic. A stag emerges from among the trees.

The failing light slides down the curve of his chest and catches in the well between his trunk and thighs, turning his fur from brown to gold. His beard lifts in the breeze. His eyes are dark and calm. His brow is crowned with dagger-like horns from which his rack ascends, curving to embrace the bowl of the sky.

His haunches are tensed. His ears swivel toward Diana, but he does not run. She longs to slide her fingers down the slope of his antlers, to their base where the softest fur grows. To press her cheek against his neck.

His head whips toward the trees, and he flicks his ears in

the direction of his gaze. She squints to see what he might be seeing, hear what he might be hearing, but her ears, even amplified, are ineffectual.

His tail quivers in warning and fans like a white flag as he darts away, one back leg pulled up to his belly.

The darkness seems to rise from the ground, obscuring her path as she follows the flash of his tail, the gleam of his antlers among far-off branches. Reeling on her spring-loaded legs, Diana trips over roots and rocks. Branches thrust between the chinks in her armored flanks, the seams that connect her parts, to scrabble at the human meat underneath.

She shakes off the assault, stumbling after the stag who melts through the trees like the stags in the Renaissance painting her father had used to teach perspective to undergraduates. In it, the deep wood teemed with bounding dogs and men and horses arched in urgency, and stags careening toward the painting's vanishing point.

The creek licks her flanks, and her hooves find purchase on the logging trail. There is the dim regularity of the field behind her house. She emerges from the woods where the cedars stand sentinel along the boundary. Her knees give out under the weight of nostalgia. The feeling of returning for summers and holidays, and in those last damaged months, to the home that had so deeply shaped her.

She could sleep in her old bed tonight, warm under the

blankets despite the spring frost. It would be so easy to take up residence in her childhood again.

She curls into the roots of the magnolia tree, breathing in the musty scent of bark that brings back to her the summer afternoons she'd wiled away in these branches. The silence is thick and pungent. In those last months with her father, she'd slept with a white noise app programmed to "Urban Rain," reminiscent of a downpour on rooftops and T tracks. The April chill digs into the gaps she'd missed when insulating her hide. Her shivering rattles her leg joints, pinching the skin behind her knees. An insect treks up her human spine, but she accepts the intrusion as the natural order of her new life. She fixes her gaze on the house, the center of her *chi*.

A light turns on inside.

The violation is breathtaking. She should barge inside and confront the trespasser. But she has not lived here in earnest for years.

The light flickers. The television, maybe, but the living room curtains are drawn shut. Her mother had sewn those curtains from a colonial pattern book—the same one her father had used to stencil the flowers on Diana's bedroom walls. As a child in bed, she had listened to her mother washing dishes and her father locking up the house, the radio on in the background.

Even as she vows to hold vigil over the house that is no longer her home, her eyes close.

In fairy tales, a stag eludes a prince, drawing him deeper and deeper into the forest. There, the prince finds a maiden: a swan princess, a sleeping beauty, a girl dressed as a beast with three dresses folded into nut shells. He finds her in a lake or a hollow tree. Although he doesn't threaten her outright, he rides a stallion and carries a bow or a gun. Often, there are dogs. He bears her back to his palace, assuming that she yearns for domestication. She grieves her wildness, even as she bears the prince's children, maybe even comes to love them.

Scents start low in the morning, ripe and full along the ground. They rise throughout the day until she wades through them, chest-high in mushroom funk, the smoky tang of moldering leaves, oily pine, sweet earthworms, her own wild oat stink. She claims certain trees, rubbing her forehead and lips against their trunks. As she gets to know the world of the woods, so she learns her own body and strives to mold her soul to it.

Three deer graze at the creek. Diana longs to be folded among their warm flanks. She hesitates, stalled by the same humbling panic that had made choosing a seat in the middle school cafeteria so daunting.

She snorts softly in welcome. The smallest doe looks up, her tail quivering in alarm. Diana meets her eyes, willing her to sense the kinship between them. The doe stamps, and the others glance up. They balk, and dart into the trees.

Diana extends her tongue-straw at the creek. The water stings her teeth. Her breath circulates inside the deer's head, the earthy odor of a refrigerator that's lost power.

She looks up, her snout dripping, to find a hound glowering at her from the opposite side of the creek. It peels back its lips, baring its teeth at Diana. Her first instinct is to run, but she's forgotten how to move the deer's legs. A whistle shrills from the direction of the house. With a snarl, the dog bounds past her, snapping at her hooves.

Though she strays ever farther from the house, Diana always circles back to it by nightfall. She sleeps below the magnolia tree in a nest of its roots. Its buds have half-split to make way for furled petals. The TV flickers in the dark. She falls asleep comforted by the light.

Her old skin swells, shoving against the new. Her feet bleed and blister; bleed again, and scab over. Shit encrusts her hind quarters. Her inner thighs are marbled with blood, her second period in the wild. Fleas ravage her scalp and pubic hair, and the sun shreds her skin where it peeks through the suit. Unceasing hiccups leave her stomachs tender. She dreams of burgers.

She lies in the creek. The current churns debris around her.

Bugs tangle in her hair. In rejecting her human body, she has become more miserably aware of it than before. The duality is disorienting, the vertigo slide of being two bodies at once.

Diana shakes dry at the creek side, rolls in moss to get the wet patches on her back. She flips to her side, savoring the length of her limbs. The stag stands a few yards away.

He turns his head sharply toward the trees, pointing his ears. His tail flips up. She follows his gaze to the logging trail, where a hunter tows a doe out of the woods. Her legs are slung over the hunter's shoulder, her long neck drags in the leaves, her open eyes are caked with dirt. The stag watches them pass by, unblinking in bland alarm. She has read that deer do not recognize death.

She charts the stag's wreckage. He's defrocked trees and shrubs, leaving ragged shreds of foliage and other scars: his incisors and antlers score the trees, his urine carves rivulets through the dirt, his hooves raze the grass. She memorizes the musk of his prints. Grinds her hooves into piles of his smooth pellets, dark and fragrant as coffee beans. Diana counts her days by glimpses of him.

Rain lashes the trees, flinging their leaves across the forest floor. Diana huddles against the magnolia tree, wincing as a gutter pipe clangs against the side of the house. The least her squatter could do is to fix the damn pipe. A growl brings her skittering to her hooves.

The hound crouches just a yard away, his ears pulled back, his tongue hanging red and wet. She looks for fear in his eyes, but there is only hunger. He scrapes his belly along the ground, whining with greed, and lunges. Diana closes her eyes.

"Heel!"

He spins in midair and lands on all fours. The hunter ducks under the tree's rain-heavy branches and grips the dog's collar, yanking him down. He turns to Diana.

She blinks back tears. The sensors taped to her eyelids open and close her deer eyes; their long fringe lashes float shut, like moths.

"What the hell are you supposed to be?" the hunter says, striking a note of wonderment. It's a woman's voice.

She wears a leather duster like the one Diana's father had worn. It had smelled like him, like shaving cream and turpentine. The huntress smells like wet dog and peanut butter. Her damp hair is gathered into a knot at the nape of her neck, and her eyes are outlined with sweeps of kohl that lends her otherwise rustic face a hint of glamor. As she takes a step toward Diana, the hound breaks free of her grip.

Diana hurtles across the stretch of yard to thicker cover. With the dog yipping behind her, she vaults over the creek in a single bound, pushing off with her hind legs and drawing her forelegs to her chest. Her breath catches, her stomach lifts in exhilaration. She imagines herself as the deer in her father's painting, plunging into the woods, pursued by snapping dogs. She revels in the reason to run.

The hound howls. As she rears to leap again, she looks back. Her body twists, and she lands on her side, tumbling into the trench. She instinctively reaches out with her hands to catch herself, but there are no hands, and she plummets, smashing her knees, her elbows, her jaw.

Diana opens her eyes to the night. Her human head feels too big, bulging against the deer's skull. Her left leg is nauseatingly hot. She moans, curling into herself to avoid witnessing the extent of the damage.

A shift in the darkness. Her eyes adjust, aching, to pick out the stag among the trees. He bows his antlers to the ground. She dreams of riding him.

Daylight filters through the branches. Her head echoes with pain. A sharper hurt digs into her hoof-seam. Her snout scrapes dirt. The stag rests beside her, the rise and fall of his breath pressing his ribs against hers. He turns his lonely eyes to her.

It occurs to her that she has never seen him with another deer. He lowers his head, gently maneuvering his antlers to the side, and nips at her hoof. He licks her ankle with his rough, warm tongue. The gentle pressure dulls the pain, calming her nausea, like the coarse washcloth her mother had used to cool her face when she was sick. The water had collected at the corners of the cloth and slid down her neck like tears.

The stag bounds ahead of Diana as she staggers out of the trench. The pain in her ankle sears up her side, making her stumble as she wades into the creek to numb her battered bodies. The water runs away with her blood.

While she rests beside the creek, the stag brings apples and flowers in his mouth and leaves them at her hooves. A dead bird. Shining candy wrappers scavenged from the huntress's trash. Diana likes the way his expressions alter his face, wariness flickering into interest, hunger pulling up the corners of his lips. She is awed by his capacity for stillness.

From the forbidden side of the creek, Diana watches the huntress watching her, kneeling on the porch with raised binoculars. The human gaze is heavy with appraisal, colored by too many shades of want. But she lets the huntress look. Being observed makes her feel closer to the stag.

Diana tries to imagine herself as the huntress sees her, up close from far away, between the fissures in her suit to the woman underneath—if there's anything left of her.

The stag's bellow rings through the trees. He mounts Diana from behind and thrusts into the suit's vaginal crevice. The impact rocks her forward; her front hooves drive into the dirt like spades, straining her wrists, vibrating up her forearms. She is docile at first, for fear of impalement, but his antlers never get in the way. She gives in to him, to her own animal desire.

Diana watches through the cover of the trees as the huntress collects her scat. The stag returns to her again and again, his tail flashing white in surrender.

The huntress places a basket of apples at the forest's edge. The dog snuffles them and growls. As the huntress watches from the porch, Diana gathers an apple between her steel-trap jaws and, tripping a spring with her tongue, crushes it in a spray of pulp. The huntress whoops, as if Diana were putting on a show. Maybe she is.

The overgrown field sparks with fireflies that illuminate the tall grass. Diana and her mother would sit in the field at night, watching. No, we can't catch them, her mother said; they should not die in captivity.

The stag rests his head against Diana's side. His eye rolls up to meet hers, and she calms in the contours of his gaze. She'd never imagined intimacy with another being could draw her closer to herself.

"I love you," she says.

He startles at the sound of her voice, rusty with disuse. She nuzzles him calm again. But she's cracked open the gap between their species, and she's not ready to close it just yet. She wants the stag to understand her fully. She tells him about the paper she'd been working on, and as she explains how to perform three-dimensional gait analysis, the stag maintains eye contact, his head tipped in interest. That's more than she could say for Kevin, who changed the subject whenever she tried to talk about work. Now, there's no one left to find her uninteresting. She'd thought that would be more freeing.

The stag's hot flank twitches, a romantic gesture to keep off the flies. She tells him about her parents and the summer nights they'd picnicked outside, and about her father's failed garden—the stag's fault, Diana reprimands him, because he'd eaten everything her father tried to grow.

But her father waited for the stag year after year, cheering when he returned after the hard frost. She tells him how her father had said he's a survivor. And how he'd watched the stag from the Adirondack chair in his last days. How the stag had helped her father have a peaceful death.

She tells him about Kevin and the life she'd left behind. How she'd started to project into the future of their life together, their house in the suburbs, their dog. She'd started to want these things—to be disappointed that she didn't have them—even at the expense of everything she'd wanted before she met him. And Kevin was right, she admitted to the stag, to herself, she *had* started to want children.

And then he'd dared to say she wouldn't compromise, although she had already compromised every part of herself. She'd already compromised just by being with him.

The stag's stiff lips shift against her tarsal gland. She welcomes his urgent warmth, and she loves him. Oh, how she loves him, although he is—and ever will remain—a mystery, while Diana has laid herself bare and found so much less mystery than she would have hoped. It's taken so little time to plumb the deepest parts of herself.

The stag comes and goes, but never far. He brings her earthworms. She can see him through the trees. Hear him in the creek. He always comes back to her.

The stag's breath is warm along her neck. She is too hot, too cold. The stag is gone, but just there, grazing in the field. It hurts to turn her head. Heavy in bloom, the magnolia drops its petals over her. The huntress stands on the logging trail, restraining the hound at her side. She's too tall for the leather duster that slaps at her knees in the wind. Her knuckles, popping against the dog's collar, are cracked. The stag surges to his hooves.

"Get up," she orders Diana.

The stag turns his ears to her, flips his tail. The hound squirms in the huntress's grip, but she holds him fast, her boots planted on either side of his belly. Diana pushes up onto her hooves, every muscle quaking. The ache has spread up her leg, her side, and into her neck. The ground tilts. The dog begins to pant.

Diana leans against the tree. For the first time, she recognizes the clumsiness of her construction, the looseness of three leg joints, the stiffness of the fourth. The stag lowers his rack at the dog and stamps his hind leg once, twice. The huntress jerks her chin at the woods.

"Run!" she commands.

The stag startles at her voice and sweeps toward the creek. Diana throbs with the need to follow, but her limbs threaten to fold.

"I can't," she says, ashamed of the despair that cracks her voice.

The huntress clicks her tongue in displeasure, and releases the hound. He bolts after the stag, yowling. Diana cannot move, cannot fall. Just leans against the tree. Her nostrils hurt, her stomach is sour. Her hide is threadbare. Her hair has fallen out in clumps.

The hound heads off the stag at the creek, crouching before him with his lips and ears back. The stag swings his antlers. They leap for each other, clash and break. The hound skitters around him, baiting him, as the stag thrusts his antlers again and again, kicking at his chest. The hound dodges his blows. Diana shouts, an involuntary, wordless exclamation that does nothing.

The hound tackles the stag's good hind leg, shaking his head, tearing at the bone. The stag stumbles, dragging the hound on his belly along the creek bed, but the stag's front legs give out and he collapses, screaming. To Diana's relief and humiliation, her senses seem altogether to fail. There is no sound, just an absence of air. She turns away, her final betrayal.

As if to comfort her, the huntress runs her palm along the planes of Diana's snout, the felted armor of her breast, the machinery of her flanks. The huntress leans in to look through the eyeholes, deep into Diana's eyes. The huntress's eyes are brown, flecked with green and pity. She hooks one finger under Diana's jaw seam.

In the fairy tales, the princess or the wild woman or the swan does not resist. She obeys because she knows she doesn't stand a chance.

The huntress cleans Diana's wounds by the living room fire. Diana lies on the Persian rug, where she'd watched TV as a child while her mother made dinner in the next room. She'd traced the patterns in its weave, the angular goats and zigzag streams, the red hills.

The huntress washes Diana's bodies and towels them dry. She administers something strong-smelling from a jar that makes her wounds burn. The huntress wraps her leg in gauze and places a pill on her tongue. Diana swallows without question.

The huntress awakens her only for more pills. She sits by Diana's head, stroking her between the ears. Details come into focus through the fog. The dog eats out of her father's cereal bowl. The huntress hangs her coat and cap on the hook by the door where Diana's father would hang his coat. It *is* his coat, she realizes.

The huntress has mounted the stag's head above the fireplace. His glass eyes look nothing like his own. The dog growls at him. At Diana.

Although nothing has changed—even her father's paintings remain on the walls—the house is made strange by the presence of the huntress. By her scent, warm and scalpy with an undertone of baking bread, a bodily, deep-down smell that emanates from between her legs, which she plants on either side of Diana as they sit by the fire, blazing despite the feverish summer heat.

The huntress wears Diana's mother's nightgown, her father's sheepskin slippers, drinks from her father's whiskey glass. She sits in Diana's father's chair in front of the TV, watching *Jeopardy*, *I Love Lucy*, and Diana's family home movies: her middle school chorus concerts and high school gymnastics routines.

The huntress kicks back with a shot of Johnnie Walker,

watching Diana's fourth birthday party. There is the unicorn cake her mother made from scratch, the crowd of kids she doesn't remember, and Diana in a white dress, ruffles brushing her bark-scraped knees.

The huntress strokes Diana's head while she dozes beside the snoring dog. There is peace in confinement.

When Diana has healed enough to stand, the huntress puts her bowl—her grandmother's wedding china—in the kitchen next to the dog's. The dog snaps at Diana when the huntress isn't looking.

The huntress oils her joints with AstroGlide. She brushes Diana's flanks and polishes her hooves. Purees lawn in the blender and adds a little something to make it more palatable: smoky mushrooms, sour berries, truffles. The huntress washes Diana's ass and thighs and applies diaper ointment to the trouble spots where suit meets skin. When Diana's eye sensors stop working, the huntress secures her eyelids open with duct tape.

As Diana becomes stronger, the huntress begins going out during the day, taking the dog with her. He wags his tongue at Diana, as if laughing.

Diana stands at the kitchen window where she'd stood as a

child. She can barely remember that Diana. Or the Diana who had brunched with Kevin on Sundays. The Diana who'd stayed late at the lab to finish up grant proposals and enjoyed it. The Diana who had watched bad TV for two weeks after calling things off with Kevin. None of those Dianas matter; none had followed her home.

The huntress begins to makes demands of Diana, entreating her to return to the wild, to find another stag for them to hunt. Diana doesn't argue; she doesn't speak. She pretends not to understand the huntress, who grips Diana's deer head between her chapped hands and bellows.

The huntress's heavy tread paces the upstairs rooms. The dog is snoring by the dying fire. Diana levels a kick at his ribs and he skitters upstairs with a yowl.

The huntress seethes with restlessness; kicks off Diana's old pink rain boots and bangs pots around the kitchen. She drinks more. She starts out earlier and comes home later.

Every night when the huntress and her dog are asleep, Diana roams the house, noticing the parts of it she'd stopped seeing when she lived here: The closet under the stairs where her mother had stored her own mother's clothing. The living room window frames gnawed by a trapped squirrel. The floorboards that creak in the middle of the night, and their constellation of knotholes. Her father's first portraits, his own family members executed in gentle strokes, tucked into corners and behind doors.

Diana relearns the house room by room, fitting it over her childhood memories whose corners still show underneath. The stag's eyes follow her mournfully, as if to say, "Is this my fate for loving you?"

The huntress brings back fireflies in mason jars and lines them on the mantle below the stag's head. She gazes at them from Diana's father's chair until they perish, one after another, like flames extinguishing.

KITE

She will not be constrained by the word "Mom," with those lines hedging in the O like a trapped breath. She prefers one M with an E like a whipping kite. She constructs a tiny house in the field behind the reservoir. She has one set of silverware, and her closet rolls out from beneath her sleeping loft. She fucks a taxi driver whose erratic hours keep her from getting bored. Her house is built on wheels. She feels alive like a soaring kite and ignores the pull from far below, as if someone were tugging the string.

BURN RUBBER

In the middle of the night, the mother empties her car onto the lawn. Goodbye, gym clothes, old car seat, clothes she's been meaning to dry clean. She crawls into the back seat, where she hasn't been since college when her boyfriend accompanied her home for spring break. They'd snuck out of her parents' house to the nature reserve parking lot. She'd gone down on him as headlights swept through the woods.

The seats are crusty. Cheez-Its grind to powder under her knees. The vacuum gasps. She scrubs the windows until she can see herself in them, the night mess of her hair. She wipes down the dash and hangs a new pine air freshener from the rearview mirror. Her fingers twitch across her nightgown. Her neighbors' houses are dark.

She uncoils the hose from the garage and swamps the car until it glistens. Turns the stream on herself, shocking her hot skin. At close range, the pressure pounds into her, but she welcomes the cleansing pain. In the morning, she will have bruises.

Bumper to bumper, she sits in silence. Her silk shirt digs into her armpits. She used to listen to NPR, but pop is easier to digest. Her brain is going dark.

Breathing deep the scent of pine, she turns on Rosetta Stone, which she never has the patience to finish. Her daughter still sings the Spanish songs she learned in daycare.

She creeps forward, flanked by indistinguishable hotel façades; chain restaurants; blank office buildings; billboards for box stores, politicians, furniture. One is blank except for the words "Your Message Here." The ruler edge of the horizon remains constant, as if she is not moving at all. In high school, she blasted Nirvana with the windows down. In college, she road-tripped thousands of miles across back roads. Now, the car shakes on the highway, and she hasn't driven above fifty in years.

She runs the noon status meeting daydreaming of speed. After her daughter was born, she was eager to get back to work where she was good at something. She'd been surprised by her aptitude for selling greeting cards. She can't remember what she'd wanted to be in college.

During her lunch hour, she tours Lincolnwood, snacking on

Danish samples from the bakery where she never buys anything. She drives through the Starbucks, and on to the park where the heaving ash trees lull her into a Zen-like state. At Borders, she browses the self-help aisle.

Bumper to bumper on the highway with the windows sealed, she screams and screams.

The lights are on in the kitchen, where her daughter is setting the table without having been asked. Only six, and already so disciplined. She wants to be an archaeologist, a circus performer, a writer, a doctor like her daddy.

Some experts say it's good for girls to have working moms. For her daughter to see her as more than just a mother. She often thinks she should struggle more with work-life balance. Her daughter's every sovereign breath has made her redundant.

She gathers the groceries, leaving one bag in the car. It contains five packages of Oreos, dry shampoo, diapers, and cherry-red Abandon lipstick she didn't pay for.

Her car's purr invades her dreams and thrums in her blood. Her husband didn't notice the bruises. They used to walk around the house naked; she'd sneak up behind him as he washed dishes and run her finger up his ass crack.

Now, she braids her daughter's hair. Packs Nora's lunch and watches out the window to make sure she gets on the kindergarten bus okay.

It's a relief to slip into the driver's seat and move toward something again.

During her lunch break, she curls up on the back seat. Rain blurs the windows. She scrapes the cream filling from an Oreo with her teeth. She is naked beneath the blanket she has stowed here. Today's silk shirt—again with too-tight sleeves—serves as a pillow. She sleeps better in the car than in her own bed, where her husband breathes too loud.

Power lines sway in the rain. She twists the top off another Oreo. Lunch hour ends. She drifts in and out of a dream about the nature reserve, the owls' gaze cutting through the car windows like headlights, the ground littered with bones. She had been afraid of her own ravenous hunger. At the beginning, she'd ride her husband until he fell asleep, and then lie awake, her body humming. It had taken years, but she'd learned to hold back. Now she's the one who turns away.

Umbrellas crowd into the rain and car doors slam around her. Tires screech on wet pavement. Headlights turn the insides of her eyelids red. She has never fully appreciated the day's slow descent. It would make a nice poem, best expressed in Spanish. She still doesn't know Spanish.

Her husband calls. She doesn't have to answer to hear his voice, the one he adopts when counseling patients. Take some time for yourself, he'd tell her. But she doesn't need his permission. She twists apart two more Oreos. She should be making dinner. Her husband was raised on meat and potatoes; Nora's a picky eater. She's forgotten what foods she likes.

The lights in the parking lot shut off. She almost wishes she'd brought a book, but it's better this way. She tries to remember how to be alone with herself.

She merges onto the highway, grinding the gas pedal into the bones of her bare foot. The car begins to rattle. At fifty, sixty, seventy, it shakes as if coming apart, groaning in the thrall of speed. She skirts the other cars. Their horns rupture the silence, the gas pedal jams against the floor. The horns fade into mournful goose calls behind her. Past her office, past her daughter's school, past her house on the cul-de-sac, waving her silk shirt out the window like a racing flag.

As the sun rises, she glides along Lake Shore Drive from Evanston's putty-colored estates to the South Side's hotels in disrepair. On her left, the lake. She turns on Rosetta Stone.

She'd planned to study abroad. Her husband promised they'd travel. But the dog—long since dead—had needed hip surgery. They'd bought a house, had a daughter, instead.

She will prevail this time, until she dreams in Spanish. In Hyde Park, she turns around and starts back up Lake Shore, repeating simple phrases. *No entiendo. ¿Te gustaría bailar conmigo? Estoy perdido. ¿Dónde está el baño?* She rolls down the windows, inviting the wind to scramble her hair. The sun heats her head, suffusing the car with the scent of scalp.

She turns on her phone just long enough to see that she has six messages and turns it off again without listening. She orders a cheese Danish with her coffee. Then two. The cashier is too chatty; her words spill across the counter and pool on the floor. She lurches back, as if to protect her shoes. The soft motor purr permeates the bakery, becoming a growl that makes her bones throb. She spins away from the cashier midsentence. The bell above the door jangles behind her as she runs for the car.

In the Borders parking lot, she watches the shoppers go in and out.

She puts on her makeup and checks into Skype for the noon status meeting, which she runs as smoothly as if she were at the conference table. Her team is convinced she's on a sales trip. While they talk, she admires how the stolen lipstick sets off her eyes.

She sleeps in the lot behind the shuttered Stop & Shop. As a teen, she and her girlfriends had hung out here for hours, smoking on the curb, daring each other to shoplift perfume. One evening, a car packed with older boys pulled up alongside them. Her friend got in and they drove away. The girls waited, shivering on the hot pavement and arguing about whether to call the police. They did nothing, until the car finally swung through the lot again, releasing their friend to the curb, giddy and glassy-eyed. She'd wondered, though never asked, what could have made her friend look that way. She pulls her blanket to her chin, breathing in the pine air.

She rockets through her neighborhood's quiet zone blasting Nirvana, flouting the ordinance she'd helped pass. Parks behind the bushes across from the elementary school. The air freshener is losing its potency. She wraps it in a tissue to preserve the last trace of pine. In its place, she hangs a coconut freshener, aura of the Caribbean. Nora gets off the bus laughing, carrying lunch, hair braided. She wants to kick the gas and slam windshield-first into the school's brick wall.

She orders at the Starbucks drive-through, then pushes on

toward the heaving ashes. She grinds the gas pedal into her foot until the car begins to shake. A rabbit darts into the road.

She swerves, splashing coffee across her legs, and careens to a stop. Tries and fails to resist looking in the rearview mirror where the stunned creature drags itself in a circle. Its hindquarters are crushed, its eyes wide and staring. She should call animal control—or put it out of its misery. She should wrap it in her silk shirt and take it to the vet. Move it out of the road, at least. She opens the door.

It's like blowing a hole in an airplane midflight. She gasps, shuddering. Her hands go white, the road breaks into static. The soft motor purr becomes a growl, then a roar of blood in her ears. The seatbelt digs into her gut. She releases the buckle, but the roaring pressure holds her fast. She pushes against it, swings her legs into the wide-open air and retches. Coffee seeps down her tan slacks. The thump of bass as another car swerves, windows down, around the rabbit and the ash trees and the children playing in the park. The roar, the smell of burnt coffee. Her pants are dry clean only.

She slams the door. The air pressure seems to level out again, and the roar quiets. Her breathing slows. She slumps against the seat, watching the rabbit crawl for the trees.

A car wash is restorative. She welcomes the thrust of the water, the slap of the rags, the heavy spurt of the hoses. When she signs the bill through the car window, she asks if they have pine air fresheners, but there's only bubblegum. She takes three.

She'd never before appreciated the accessibility of everyday things: coffee, cash, fast food, gas. If only bathrooms had drive-through, and liquor stores. She pays strangers to buy her white wine and pees in Tupperware. She tosses her toilet paper at the edge of the park. Scrubs her armpits with baby wipes and washes her hair out the window, dry shampoo flaking onto the pavement. Dental gum strips the grit from her teeth. She finds drive-through salads inadequate, but needs the nutrients. She makes the most of what she has, like those shows about confronting the wild with nothing more than a ball of string and a tarp.

She turns down unfamiliar streets, only to end up on the highway again.

The radio dies. At first, she welcomes the silence. Then, she becomes aware of her stomach gurgling, her throat constricting. She forgets to breathe and sighs in gusts. The air conditioner whistles. The brake pedal squeaks. Something rattles in the back, but she can't find its source.

She stops for hitchhikers, just for conversation. Some ask

what happened to her, and she pretends not to speak English. She only takes them as far as the state line.

She watches the shoppers go in and out until Borders closes. She must have missed the status meeting. She hoards her lipstick in the glove compartment. Behind the shuttered Stop & Shop, she sleeps deeply now.

Nora gets off the bus. Braids, lunchbox, backpack. She used to want to paint every day after daycare. She'd squeeze out all the colors and mix them into gray with her fingers. "Paint with me, Mama," she'd demand. She'd painted anything her daughter wanted.

In the last year, Nora had decided she'd rather draw with pencils, by herself. She sat beside her daughter, waiting for a moment she might be useful, her hand on Nora's back.

She sits long after the buses clear. Her diaper is wet, but hasn't reached capacity. She's down to one roll of toilet paper. Out of gum.

Bumper to bumper, she cracks the window. It draws in exhaust from the truck ahead.

When she takes the car for an oil change, the mechanic asks her to wait in the lobby. There's a television and a coffeepot, he says, as if to tempt her. When she says she'd prefer to stay in the car, he just shakes his head and steps aside so she can drive onto the platform. She rises like a Viking maiden on a funeral pyre.

Past hotel facades, chain restaurants, blank offices, billboards, toward the ruler edge of the horizon. She should bust through the state line and drive until she runs out of gas, until she stumbles from the bowels of the car onto unfamiliar ground. Instead, she exits toward Starbucks, Borders, the heaving ashes.

Diapers fester on the back seat. Hitchhikers refuse rides. Her teeth are loose, and she doesn't remember the last time she Skyped into work. She has become intimate with the sweet and sour scent of her body, her moldering, below ground stink. Her breath, her greasy scalp, her moist armpits and ripening vagina, like sourdough bread baking.

She parks across from the school as the buses line up, their windows fogged with breath. The doors open, and as the kids step off the bus, she almost expects them to go up in flames the second they touch the ground. She grips the wheel, but they file onto the sidewalk and drag their feet toward school. The doors close without her daughter.

She doesn't remember the last time she turned on her phone. She digs it out of a tissue mound, but the battery's dead.

Nora is home sick, or missed the bus, or she was plucked from the sidewalk by a carful of boys. A motherless child is easy prey.

The last bubblegum air freshener has faded. Her legs stick to the seat. Her fingers are puffy on the wheel, her nails ragged. She avoids her face in the rearview mirror.

Her house is dark. She inches forward, scraping the lawn, straining to see into the living room window that only reflects her own car. It would be so easy to slip inside. She could take a shower, eat a hot meal, watch TV.

Nora appears on the front steps. She is wearing pajamas. Her feet are bare, her cheeks flushed. Her hair feathers around her head. She looks a little lost, as though she's been sleepwalking. Ever disciplined, she remains on the steps. She is not allowed out of the house alone. Rocks on her heels, regarding the car like a wary animal.

It's good for girls to learn self-sufficiency, to have ambitious moms. She should scoop Nora into the house and administer chicken soup and flat ginger ale. They'd watch cartoons, and she'd curl protectively around Nora's body, pressing it into her own. She should turn off the ignition. Apologize, at least.

Push back against the roar. But if she gets out, it will mean she has arrived.

She hits the locks and tears off the lawn, grinding the gas pedal into her foot until it aches.

As she rounds the cul-de-sac, she tries and fails to resist looking in the rearview mirror where Nora is running across the raw lawn. Running for the road.

THE TENANT

The bear rifles through my garbage. He steals my newspaper and dozes in my magnolia tree. He helps himself to the cat's food, dipping his paws into the dish, his ears twitching. Last night, he stood off with a raccoon. When it dug its fingers into the food, the bear popped its head off. It was only that once, though. He was staking his claim.

As he performs laps in the aboveground pool, I keep still on my inflatable raft. He sprawls in my lounge chair with his belly to the sun. We sunbathe in companionable silence.

When the pool is covered, he comes to my door. I keep the screen locked now that Frank is gone. The bear looks at me with heavy-lidded eyes shadowed with soft, damp fur. I unlock the screen and let him in.

He follows my tour with polite interest and particularly likes the den, where Frank used to watch football and read the paper. He climbs into Frank's easy chair, and when I show him how it reclines, he snuffles with pleasure.

It's good to hear the game downstairs again while I make supper. I prepare salmon fillets with lemon and dill and serve them on TV trays so we can eat together in the den. He sniffs the fish, his claws clinking against the plate, and polishes it off in two bites.

As I clear his tray, he roars. I drop to the carpet and play dead. When nothing happens, I look up to find him watching me with a quizzical expression. His team lost, is all.

I sleep well now. If a thief or a rapist broke in, the bear would pop his head off. We try all kinds of fish. He likes the bottom-feeders best. They taste like dirt, but I defer to his preference. Frank didn't like fish. He had a meat and potato palate. The bear will eat anything I make with relish. I learn to bake, poach, fry, batter, sear, and soufflé. The bear's coat is getting thick and glossy. We eat by candlelight.

New magazines arrive: *Field & Stream*, *Ranger Rick*, seed catalogues, the *New Yorker*. He keeps the room tidy. I've never seen him do his business, though I've heard the den toilet flush.

He sleeps in the easy chair rolled up in my grandmother's afghan with his nose sticking out. Sometimes when I can't sleep, I lie on the couch that still smells like Frank, and talk to the bear. I tell him what I'm reading these days. I tell him what's happening in the Middle East. I tell him how Frank and I met in college, when I'd planned to be a journalist. How I followed Frank here and never went to the Middle

East, and now I struggle to make small talk at the grocery store. People's eyes glaze over when I talk. Frank was the only one who listened.

The snow rises against the windows. It rises so high it covers the aboveground pool. We have everything we need right here. The den is dark and full of bear breath. The meaty smell is comforting in its own way. Sometimes, I sit on the floor between the bear's paws, and he rests his chin on my head. Heat rolls off him in woolly waves. His ears twitch in his sleep.

The trees sparkle as the snow slips off, leaving their branches raw. I dip my feet into a puddle of sunlight spreading across the bedroom floor. Warm breath nuzzles the back of my neck, and claws curve along my clavicles. The bed sags under his weight. He looks at me with a hungry gleam in his eyes.

I make pancakes, eggs, bacon, hash browns, and coffee. When the bear is finished, he lumbers outside. I do the dishes, a little resentful that he doesn't help.

It's still cold for the pool, but I fill it anyway and watch as he performs laps in the ice blue water. Reclining in the lounge chair, he trims articles from the paper with his claws. He dozes in my magnolia tree and rifles through my garbage. He steals a jacket from my neighbor's laundry line and helps himself to the cat's food. He does not come back inside. I leave the screen door unlocked, just in case.

There's a knock, but it's not the bear. The man on the porch asks about this spring we're having, and when I ask him if he's been following the refugee crisis, he says he'll just get to the point. The bear has listed me as a reference. He seems like a quiet and respectful bear, and he has passed the credit check. In my experience, would I recommend him as a tenant?

The bear could have stayed with me as long as he wanted. But maybe he's tired of my company. Maybe he'd prefer stainless steel appliances. Or room for a family. I could say the bear is untidy and has a temper, and maybe then he'll come home.

His snout pokes around the pool, and he looks at me with damp eyes. He is wearing Frank's tie.

The bear is pleasant enough, I say. He has never eaten anyone or upset my garbage cans. He is careful not to puncture the pool with his claws, so I think he would be respectful of hardwood floors. I do not tell the man about the raccoon.

I keep the screen door locked, but I stock up on bottom-feeders just in case. As the snow rises past my windows, I watch television wrapped in my grandmother's afghan that still smells like bear. When I lose power, I pile all the blankets and towels onto the bed and sleep under them. It's warm, but I can't breathe.

PAINT BY NUMBER

My mother painted birds by number at the home for elegantly aging widows. In art school when she met my father, she refused to fall in love. She wore feathered hats and painted mountains on blank city walls. But she followed my father to Iowa though the land was so damn flat. She cleaned and cooked and sketched the masterpieces she would paint. Queen of the cornfields, she made hats for scarecrows. The crows landed at her feet. "I'm invisible," she said. When my father called her *Mama*, I wished she'd say, "I have a name." His colleagues introduced themselves every time they met. "It's like I'm invisible," she said. Grocery carts grazed her shins. "I'm invisible," she said. At the home, she began to paint by number and to wait. She disappeared on Meatloaf Monday.

THE MONSTER AT MARTA'S BACK

Jim does not hold Marta's hand over the gearshift. The muscle in his jaw twitches. Its appearance, heralding his temper, used to terrify the girls. Marta rarely sees it now that they're grown. As they pull up at the train station, the bo staff rolls in the back.

The parking lot is empty, and the platform lamps do little to ease the winter darkness. On any other day, she would find the deserted station melancholy.

She doesn't care what Jim says; she is not bringing a weapon on the train. No one will bother an old lady. No one notices her anyway.

"I left some dinners in the fridge," she tells Jim again, fighting to keep the excitement from her voice. She made ten meals, one for each day she'll be in Baltimore. The last time Jim cooked was thirty-five years ago when, early in their courtship, he'd seared a steak on a bed of salt. They had laughed over the inedible husk and ordered out. In subsequent years, she wondered if he ruined the steak on purpose so he'd never have to cook again.

That isn't fair. He works hard and comes home every night, while she hasn't had a job since graduate school. Even then, she was just a nanny. She's had other things to do, of course: managing their home, raising Cora and Becca, cooking, laundry, grocery shopping. She had paved the way for her daughters to have it all.

Marta already has her coat on, since Jim keeps the car so cold. He sweats when he drives. She waits for him to say he's proud of her, to "knock 'em dead," to "be careful and have fun"—all the things he told Cora and Becca when they left for college, studied abroad, started their first jobs. She waits for Jim to look at her. He keeps his hands on the wheel. She twists the strap of her new leather satchel around her wrist.

She won't tell Jim she's scared. She'd called Cora for reassurance, but Cora had refused to offer it because her therapist says seeking reassurance provides only temporary relief, and then the worry comes back stronger than before. "So, I'm going to stop reassuring you," Cora said.

Marta used to reassure Cora when she worried about home invasion and bad grades and making friends.

"You shouldn't have reassured me," says Cora, who is determined not to pass on her anxiety to her own daughter. As if Marta could have vanquished it, and failed.

Becca would say she inherited her confidence from Jim.

Her daughters always attribute their strong qualities to their father: their work ethic, their punctuality and sense of direction. They blame Marta for their worry, their awkwardness, the projects they leave unfinished.

"I'll just wait in the station," she says. She can't remember the last time she spent so much as a night away from Jim. He stares at the platform, open to the tracks. Marta kisses the twitching muscle in his jaw, but he doesn't budge. She shoulders her satchel, lifts her suitcase out of the trunk. She'll have to carry it herself the rest of the trip, anyway. She waves from the station door, but Jim just drives off.

The winter air keeps her tears at bay. The news is on inside, where a man is sleeping across a row of plastic seats. Though her fingers and toes are already going numb, Marta drags her suitcase to the end of the platform and claims the last bench.

She packed a granola bar for the train, but forgot her soda in the car, she realizes now with a start of fear. She has already forgotten something. Jim is probably rolling his eyes. Maybe he'll bring her the soda—but she knows he won't. It's her own damn fault, and she'll just have to go thirsty now. She hopes he won't come back. She'd be too tempted to let him take her home.

She resists the urge to text him an apology for leaving the soda in the car. She doesn't know why she's sorry.

"I miss you already," she writes. "I love you."

Jim only recently learned to text and sends long messages to their daughters signed, "Dad." He never writes to Marta.

The man emerges from the station at the far end of the platform and rocks forward to peer down the tracks. Coarse red hair curls around his cheeks and bursts from his shirt collar. He doesn't have a suitcase.

Marta checks her satchel for her train ticket. Here it is, tucked into the manila folder with her manuscript pages.

"We are pleased to offer you a spot with twenty other exceptional writers," the email said. For her application, she had resurrected the novel she'd abandoned when Cora was born, about a queen who builds a labyrinth to trap a Minotaur. She'd planned to keep writing, to defend her voice against the patriarchy. But after the birth of her daughters, she didn't have time—and everything she had to say seemed small.

The novel's first line still gives her a shiver of promise, transports her back to the campus coffee shop where it sprang into her brain and demanded she pursue it.

She casts her attention inside herself, and is relieved to find a deep need there, like a stomachache. She's eager to rewrite the pages. They are too grandiose, too preachy. She has come to appreciate short sentences.

Marta is ready. She has her resurrected manuscript and five pens. She has her clothes and her laptop. That's all she needs.

The man starts down the platform toward her with a

strange strutting gait. He won't bother an old lady. No one notices her anyway.

At Jim's work parties, the other lawyers and their wives, whom she's known for thirty years, always forget her name. People cut in front of her in line. Yesterday at the pharmacy, when she pointed out that she'd been at the counter first, her interloper said, "No need to get mad." She hadn't been mad, but men always think an assertive woman is bitchy. That's what she tells her daughters. Though Becca actually is a little bitchy.

Her youngest called at one o'clock this morning to complain about another boyfriend. She *knows* he's on the road with his band, but he could spare five fucking seconds to text "I love you."

When Becca swears, Marta feels like she failed as a mother. Then again, Cora *never* swears, and she could stand to grow a backbone. Marta has failed her, too.

The man passes all the other benches until only Marta's is left. She doesn't have anything valuable, except her laptop and the cab money Jim gave her—but the man wouldn't know that. She rolls her suitcase tight against her thigh. In graduate school, she rode trains all over Chicago and was never even groped.

It's unthinkable now that she and Jim had lived in a city, much less Chicago's South Side. When the owner of their favorite diner was killed in a drive-by, she and Jim had left ten-dollar bills in the tip jar for his wife and kids. That was the closest they'd come to violence, until a gang of teens bashed their neighbor in the head with a two-by-four. They cracked his skull, but it gave him something to write about. His poetry has been published in the *New Yorker*. Nothing like that has ever happened to Marta. That's why she's never been published.

The man sits beside Marta. She eyes him without turning her head. Sharp buds of horns jut through his wiry hair.

Jim wouldn't admit to worrying, but he'd monitored the news for racial unrest all month, sharing the most terrifying incidents over dinner. He painted a vision of Baltimore ruled by looters and drug lords, a wasteland inhospitable to writing retreats.

On his way to pick up Becca at the Greyhound station last month, he had grabbed her old bo staff from the closet.

"Just in case," he said, sliding it onto the back seat.

Marta doubted he could wield a stick against an angry mob. *He* hadn't studied karate, like Becca. But it didn't matter; there were no protestors at the station. And if there *had* been protestors, they wouldn't have been intimidated by Jim in his boaters and salmon shirt. Becca teased him on the drive home from the station. She lives in New York and yells at cab drivers.

The man begins to file his fingernails, long and sharp as claws, dusting Marta's trousers with shavings. People have so little consideration for others. Becca would just tell him to fuck off. She is awe-inspiring, with her independence and entitlement. Her confidence on public transportation. She makes herself heard at meetings and takes credit for her ideas. She demands promotions. Cora is more like Marta. She's held the same job for ten years because she's waiting for someone else to tell her she deserves more.

Marta tries to help, advises her to "Figure out what you want, and go for it." But Cora just shuts her down. "Take your own advice," she says.

They haven't had this talk for a while, but Marta suspects her daughter hasn't changed. Cora has just stopped telling her things.

As he finishes filing, the man blows on the tip of each claw, engulfing Marta in his hot, oniony breath.

It was Cora who sent her the application for the residency and pestered her until she filled it out. Marta humored her, figuring she'd never be accepted. Hundreds of writers apply, writers with real credentials.

"The residency is for *emerging* writers," Cora said.

Funny to think she could still be emerging at anything. When she got the acceptance email, she didn't tell anyone for three days.

"They must not have had many applicants this year," she told Cora. "Anyway, I can't go. You know your dad . . ."

"Dad can make his own dinner," Cora said.

Cora and her husband split their chores. Sometimes, when Cora has a hard day at work, Greg even makes dinner. The baby spends nine hours at daycare.

It would be rude to move to a different bench, so she'll wait a few minutes, then nonchalantly walk down the platform as if stretching her legs.

It was a different time when Marta was a new mother. She'd kept her girls busy with art projects, games, outings to the aquarium and the playground, and when they'd been everywhere else, to the airport to watch the planes take off. She'd made dinner—two different meals because the girls were picky and Jim wouldn't eat chicken fingers. If she'd sent the girls to daycare, maybe she'd have been a real writer. Marta hasn't done anything for herself since 1979. Or so Cora says.

Now that Cora is a mother, she passes judgment on everything Marta did wrong. The sacrifices she shouldn't have had to make. Marta defends her choices: "They didn't have daycare when you were little," and "That's just the way your father is." But Jim didn't thank her for the dinners. Not today—not any day for the last thirty-five years.

Marta prepares to make her escape. She stretches one leg, then the other, and sighs in soul-deep exhaustion she doesn't have to fake. The man yawns, his red tongue unrolling between his fangs like a rug. Marta's palms slide on her satchel. She stands and peers down the platform as if looking for someone at the station. Her fingers are shaking with cold, their tips white below the nail. It's not too late to call Jim. She'd apologize, and he would hold her hand over the gearshift on the way home.

Marta tried to find the ideal moment to tell him about the residency, but there was no right time. She usually begins talking as soon as he comes home from work—a habit that had taken hold when she was alone with the babies all day, starved for conversation. She follows him upstairs where he changes, to the hall cabinet where he pours a scotch, to the living room where he stands watching TV, half-listening to her until she says, "You're not listening to me," and when he makes no effort to disagree, she retreats to the kitchen to make dinner. She shouldn't get so frustrated, she chides herself; she doesn't have anything to say, anyway.

She told Jim about the residency over dinner. Almond-crusted pork loin on a bed of mashed potatoes with lemon-garlic green beans. She told him she'd applied on a whim, that she knew it was too far away and she was too old. Jim didn't say a word. He didn't have to—she was preempting his arguments.

"What do you think?" she asked, finally.

"About what?"

He knew she wouldn't go. That she was just talking to fill space.

But she *did* have something to say, damn it. At least, the residency judges thought so. They thought her twenty pages were strong enough to offer her room and board, to call her a "valuable addition to a cadre of talented writers." Although she told Jim she was going, it's possible he didn't believe her until they arrived at the station.

Behind her, the man stands up, too. She begins to walk toward the station, as if expecting someone to emerge. Jim hasn't responded to her text. Her breath plumes before her. They used to try new things. They'd gone camping and skiing. Eaten in dives and stayed at motels. They'd changed each other, probably—grown into each other. But Jim still goes to work. He has parts of himself that belong just to him. Marta sometimes wonders who she'd be if she had guarded herself better.

Her bag drops from her numb fingers, spilling her manuscript and granola bar and pepper spray onto the concrete. Her pens roll toward the tracks and she loses sight of them in a blur of tears. The man stands at her back, his breath sawing at her neck. The train whistle blasts across the platform. She's made a terrible mistake.

She snatches up the pepper spray, wishing she'd brought the bo staff. Becca knows how to land a punch. The poet didn't have a chance to fight back. He crawled into the lobby of their building, where he would have died if the janitor hadn't found him.

As the train rounds the tracks, she pivots and, startled by her own guttural shout, releases the safety lock on the pepper spray. A cloud sears the air. The man cries out, pawing at his eyes. Marta holds her breath and scoops her bag off the ground as the train screams to a stop. She runs.

Jim hasn't responded to her text. Hasn't thanked her for the dinners. Didn't even congratulate her on the residency. But he snuck pepper spray into her bag.

A door opens just ahead. Marta flies toward it, driven by the hot breath at her back. Her suitcase nips at her heels. She runs for her life.

STONE FRUIT

Alice had wanted to sleep beneath the stars nestled in a gypsy's arms. She'd wanted to travel the world and write a novel rivaling *War and Peace*. Now, she wants a house to grow old in.

She still wants to make something beautiful. She wants a miniature greyhound, and a garden for it to dig in. She wants stainless steel appliances. She knows the ache of desire. She waits for the ache to come for a child, but it does not. Her husband talks of one with his blue eyes and her curly hair. She cannot see this child. She is jealous that he can.

She checks for the ache daily. Alice and her husband have long talks that leave her resentful. She does not want responsibility for his happiness. When she pushes him away, she laughs to lessen the blow.

He calls her from work one afternoon. Just below his window, an old man folded to the grass and lay on his back staring up at the sky. Leaves landed on his face. The paramedics came, but there were no sirens. The story holds everything he wants her to understand.

That night, she climbs on top of him, and his look of surprised gratitude is almost too much to bear. She is full and afraid. He cups her belly in his hands.

She cannot feel anything. Not yet. But they tell her it's there. Cells knitting together, blood vessels spidering out, neurons sparking. She trips over nothing, thinking of the child. She digs her fingers into her belly, feeling for it.

She hopes the ache will grow inside her slowly, along with the child. The months pass, but the ache does not come, and the child does not grow. Alice's relief is tempered by her husband's disappointment.

They find joy in other things. They travel. They drink interesting cocktails. They buy a home they can't afford. But she sees the way his eyes follow families, how he smiles to himself, warm and distant. He does not share this smile with her. Sometimes Alice's body is weighed down by what it has not made. She writes a novel. They save for retirement. She learns to live with the heaviness. They adopt a greyhound. She writes more novels.

When her husband dies at fifty-five, the heaviness sets in for good. Grief grows inside her, gathering cells, growing fingernails. The heaviness gets so bad she can barely walk.

The doctor sends signals into her depths, and she is awed by the cavernous shadows that gather on the screen. They make her body all the more mysterious to her. Alice feels for the ache of desire out of long habit, and finds a deep, strange tenderness instead. Yes, just there, where the shadows are gathering. She has carried it all these years. The size of a fist, it is ridged with muscle and vein, solid as stone.

ANIMAL WIFE REVISITED

The swans follow the restless wind. It fattens in spring, rolls over fields and between mountains, and fasts in winter until it is lean and snapping. When the wind flies into a rage, the swans shield one another with their wings. Clouds cling to their feathers and trail like ghosts behind them. They drift with the river deep into the forest, spinning around patches of ice, content to go where the wind takes them—except the youngest, for whom drifting isn't enough.

She longs to race in a sled and sleep cloaked in furs by a fire. She yearns to ride the wheel on the pier, its lights sparking against the night sky. She watches the children clambering stone to stone on the jetty, collecting crabs with shining backs. She dreams of the person she would be: a little girl with wild hair and greedy eyes.

Her sisters say no good can come of longing. They move on, their wings like billowing sails. But longing draws the youngest swan from her sisters at night. She ventures farther and farther from them, returning with the sun. The wind tries to face her down. She grows tired and heavy, but still she pushes on.

She crosses deserts where men travel on strange beasts. The wind casts sand in her eyes, but still she pushes on, above a town choked with trees, where wedding guests gather in a churchyard. Stone walls stitch the land together. She longs to join the children playing on the riverbank, but when she opens her wings to them, they run from her.

She returns to her sisters with dirty feet, her long neck drooping. The wind strums her feathers, but she digs into the brush and tucks her head. She sighs so bitterly that her sisters defy the wind and lead her to a pond sheltered by trees tall as masts. The morning smells like pine, rainwater, musk of bears. They will give her one day only, until the sun sets.

How will one day be enough, she laments, as the swans strip their feathered robes. The sun mocks her from the tree-tops, turning the forest gold. She wades into the pond with human legs that are too long and shapely. She has missed childhood.

As the sun licks her bare shoulders, she shivers with the knowledge that she will never again feel its weight on her skin. She flinches as the pond laps at her breasts, thinking already of night.

The forest burns from gold to red, silent but for her sisters' laughter. It turns red to blue between black branches, and she closes her eyes against the creeping night.

Her skin blazes, drawing the water to steam. In her eagerness, she had flung her feathers over a branch. A man stands at the pond's edge, clutching them to his chest. She can feel his hands on her skin. Her sisters pull their feathers around their shoulders. The man's arms tighten.

The sun ducks behind the trees. Her sisters cry for her to join them, beating the man with their wings, but still he holds tight to her feathers. The wind churns the forest into frenzy as her sisters leave her behind.

She follows the man, clothed in nothing but darkness. She has no choice; he holds her soul in his hands. His house is bare, though he has lived here all his life, he says. He wraps a blanket around her shoulders. He is kind, and she cannot refuse him. She asks for her feathers, and he kisses her instead.

Every morning she asks for her feathers, and every morning he kisses her, until she stops asking. She has a little room for sewing or painting or spinning flax into gold. She stands at the window instead, palms pressed to her belly.

Her husband brings home flowers and she listens as he talks about his day. He unrolls blueprints for new houses. He builds a cradle. When the baby is born with feathers, the man lies awake at night worrying she will fly away. He hides her feathers, too.

The mother holds her up to things. Books, she says, running her daughter's hands along their spines. Sky, she points out the window of her little room. Hot, she holds the baby over boiling water until her cheeks are red. When she runs out of things to name, she tells her daughter why she loves her. She starts with the way she knots her fingers before her face. The rim of gray around her blue irises. Her joyful shriek upon glimpsing her reflection.

Happiness has sharp edges. At night, she rests her palm on the baby's chest. Its rise and fall is so faint she presses harder, until the baby thumps her legs in protest. The nights are long and quiet. She often wakes searching for her daughter among the pillows.

On the first day of kindergarten, she rediscovers herself in the empty house and finds there is nothing left. She does the dishes and the laundry. When the dishes and the laundry are done, she mops the floor. She dirties dishes just so she can wash them again.

She does not leave the house. Her skin turns so pale her veins shine through it like rivers.

The girl does homework at the kitchen table and talks of things her mother doesn't understand. She writes in her journal, shielding the page with one hand. Dodges her mother's lips. She is a fine girl with wild hair and greedy eyes.

The mother sits at the table, waiting for the oven timer to go off. Her daughter gusts through the door, tracking mud across the kitchen. She will need to mop again. The girl places a box between her hands. It has no latch, no key. The mother recognizes her husband's handiwork. The oven timer buzzes. Her fingers shake as she lifts the box. The oven timer buzzes. The wind batters the windows, trying to reach her.